GUARDIAN ANGEL.

MEMOIRS

OF A

GUARDIAN ANGEL.

Translated from the French of

M. L'ABBÉ G. CHARDON,

Honorary Canon, Superior of the Diocesan Mission of
Clermont-Ferrand.

BALTIMORE:

PUBLISHED BY JOHN MURPHY & CO.

NEW YORK: ... CATHOLIC PUBLICATION SOCIETY.
BOSTON: ... PATRICK DONOHOE.
1871.

APPROBATION.

 WE have had the "MEMOIRS OF A GUARDIAN ANGEL" carefully examined, and We approve of the same, as a work which is well calculated to foster faith and piety among the faithful.

Baltimore, Feast of St. Cecilia, Nov. 22, 1870.

THOMAS S. LEE,
Secretary.

MARTIN J. SPALDING,
Archbishop of Baltimore.

Preface of the Translator.

THE translation of this work was undertaken at the request of one of the most zealous of our Prelates, and with the full consent of the Author. The only condition required by the latter was, that the references at the foot of each page, in the French, should be retained in the English edition. One of the charms of this book is the adaptation Rev. M. Chardon makes of facts found narrated in the Lives of the Saints by approved writers; and as some of these facts are of such a nature as almost to surpass imagination, it is well the reader should see that the Author in so delicate a matter is not indulging his fancy. The maxims of spiritual and ascetical life are drawn from the best sources, and are skilfully interwoven in the memoirs.

Speaking of this book, the *Monde*, of July 24th, 1870, says: "A touching and inspiring subject. It has been treated a hundred times in every manner, and yet M. Chardon has found a way of being new — in constantly taking his stand on the doctrine of the Fathers, of the safest mystical writers, and principally on the examples, words, and revelations of Saints of both sexes. This, in our opinion, is the only path to tread, to succeed in the matter of books of devotion, and avoid the commonplace nullities that inundate us. We cordially thank the Abbé Chardon for having so happily guarded against adding to the number."

This book is worthy of remark for other reasons. It shows that Catholicity is ever alive to the wants of the age. 'T is not a thing of the past, but is always of the present. In this epoch, when superstition is tending, especially among us, to take the place of religion, the Church, in one of her sons, lays before all the true idea of that spiritual agency on our life, which no amount of stolid indifference or materialism can make us ignore. Again, this work will be useful to those who have turned their attention to spiritism; it will show them what they are to believe, according to approved experience, and the dangers they are exposed to, in trifling with powers far beyond their control.

To Catholics the book will recommend itself.

ROME, July, 1870.

Author's Preface.

THESE Memoirs are a gallery of paintings in which is brought into view the Catholic doctrine on the ministry of Guardian Angels.

An Angel here tells what were his duties and his impressions from the moment in which a soul was intrusted to him, to that in which she took her place at his side in glory.

We see at a glance, what this best of friends has done for us in the past, is doing for us now, and will do for us in the future.

May the reading of these pages excite the gratitude of hearts that receive so many benefits, and lead them to correspond with these more faithfully! This is the end which the Author had in view.

Contents.

viii

CONTENTS.

MEMOIRS OF

A GUARDIAN ANGEL.

I.

Expectation.

ROM the day when it was told me I was to be a Guardian Angel, I burned with impatience. The time seemed long ere I could leave and go to the earth to do my work of mercy.

In heaven I could not taste such happiness. There all tears are wiped away, all labors are ended.*

* S. Augustin, Comment. on the 148th Psalm.

2

The earth offered a vast arena to my zeal. Misery abounds there; it is its own country, and its place of birth.*

The Creator had set an example of compassion, in visiting, after their fall, men who had sinned. The angels had darted down to follow Him, and were running in the way He had traced out for them.†

"To save a soul," they said, "to make forever happy a creature endowed with intellect and feeling, to give to God one more worshipper for all eternity, to prepare for ourselves and our country a true and grateful friend—what a privilege! Will not our happiness be increased thereby, even in the bosom of infinite delights? ‡

The Incarnation put the finishing stroke to this charity. In raising souls to a new dignity, it had made a new kind of love spring up in the hearts of their heavenly guardians.

* Bossuet, Sermon on Guardian Angels
† Origen, Homily I on Ezechiel
‡ Bossuet, Sermon sur les Anges Gardiens

God had, from the beginning, allotted to pure spirits their labors; to some, that of seeking the general good of mankind; to others, that of watching each over one soul.* Of these latter I was one. On the advent of a soul whom God alone saw in the future, my ministry was to commence. At what time, in what place, under what auspices was she to appear? I knew not.

Without having seen her, I loved her already, and my affection did not cease to grow in proportion as the wished-for term drew near.†

When an infant was born on earth, I flew to the throne of God, and, like each one of my brothers, I hastened to say to Him, "Will it be I, Lord, who shall have the honor of guiding it on its pilgrimage?"

* Bail., Théologie Affective, des Anges.
† Boudon, Dévotion aux Neuf Chœurs des Anges

II.

The First Sight.

MY turn came. A new babe was born. The Most High made a sign. . . . I was the happy chosen one.*

Without delay I flew to my pupil. The angel of its mother had guarded it till then. Protector of the tree, he watched over the fruit that hung on its branch. But on opening its eyes to the light, the infant was to be given to me.† After having awaited it for so long a time, I found it at last. I stretched out my arms to it; I was going to press it to my

---

* St. Jerome, Commentary on St. Matthew.
† St. Thomas, Treatise on the angel's guest, 113, art. 5.

heart. . . . Bitter deception! The sight checked my movement. The Divine likeness scarcely shone in this soul. A hideous leprosy disfigured her. She had the stain of her origin.

Two opposite feelings strove within me: profound pity for a soul so dear, invincible horror of her defilement.*

"She is mine!" said Satan. "She has entered into life only to fall into my power. Behold the seal of malediction! She belongs to that race of proscribed ones who owed to me once their fall, and who owe to me daily their misfortunes." †

How critical was the situation of this little infant! A too sudden movement, a fall, a mere nothing . . . and behold this frail existence shattered! behold an immortal soul exiled to those places the light of the Divine Face will never illumine. Satan knew it;

* Life of St Sebastian, Bollandists
† Tertullian, Treatise on the Soul

2 *   B

he would have wished to snatch it from life in a moment; he would not have feared to strike the fatal blow. But his power went not that far. I was to put a limit to his cruelty.*

While he was suggesting to the relatives a thousand pretexts for deferring the baptism, or seeking to deceive their vigilance, I kept alive their solicitude, and communicated to them the ardor of my zeal.†

* Jacques Marchant, Jardin des Pasteurs.

† Lives of SS. Thyrsus and Bassianus, Boll. Bondon, Devot. to the Nine Choirs of Angels.

III.

The Baptism.

THE child was presented at the sacred font. I was full of joy. It seemed to me that I was myself about to receive some great favor.*

"Flow, regenerating water! spread thyself upon its brow; and may I see as soon as possible its soul such as my love desires."

But no. . . . Standing face to face with Satan, the minister of Jesus Christ will not send away the usurper without humbling him.

* St. J. Chrysostom, Sermon on the Ascension. St. Thomas Villavona, Sermon on the Angels.

Under the veil of the exorcisms, I saw the priest chain him, scourge him, pierce him with darts. What cries that angel of evil uttered! Each anointing lit up within him the fire of a new hell.*

The priest gave him only the withering names of unclean spirit, of spirit worthy of damnation, of damned spirit. He recalled to him the anathema he incurred, the second judgment he is to undergo, the increase of woe that awaited him, and forced him to give glory to the Father, Son, and Holy Ghost.†

The water flowed at last. What virtue in a drop of water! All the wonders of grace were contained in it. From the instant it touched the brow of the new-born infant there were no stains, no malediction and, no death. Satan had fled swift as lightning; the Spirit of Love had come down, and from heaven

---

* St Cyprian, Letter to Magnus St. Basil Cæsar, Homily on Humility. Life of St Mary Magdalen de Pazzi, Boll

† Ceremonies of Baptism.

a voice made itself heard, "This is my child." *

For this child of men become a child of God, everything had changed: it was called by a new name, a new family had adopted it, a new life circulated in its members. To sin had succeeded grace. From the hands of Satan, it had just passed into the hands of an angel.†

Nothing was indifferent to its happiness. The fingers of the elect had swept the harps of gold, and in hell the demons had roared. Two souls, that had just made for it a profession of faith, looked on it as their child, and from the borders of its country a saint had bent toward the exile and said, " I will be thy protector." ‡

* St Matthew, III Tertullian, Tract on Baptism Life of St Mary d'Oignies, Boll
† Origen, Hom in Ezechiel. Life of St Bassianus, Boll
‡ St. Gregory Naz., on Baptism Life of St Geneviève, Boll

IV.

The Crib.

ON the return from the temple I helped to carry the child. I hastened to bless its crib. Its mother placed it there, after having fondly kissed it with religious respect. I watched like herself over this dear treasure. My wings were folded over it and protected its slumber. Its eyelid opened and closed under my look. The beating of its heart filled me with joy.*

"Sleep, sleep, under the wing of thy angel. There hast thou nothing to fear; thou art at the threshold of paradise.

* Louis of Blois, Retreat of the Faithful Soul.

22

"What charms does a smile of Divine goodness give to the humblest of creatures!

"'Tis that makes from foul clay bud forth daily the rose and the lily.

"Come! O my brothers in heaven; the earth has spectacles worthy of you.

"Here, in the darkness, is the star of a day destined to shine for eternity.

"Under these bonds, and in this frail body, you can contemplate your most beautiful image." *

Thus, by the couch where innocence slept, I sang the riches of grace.

I could not resist the joy of giving an outward mark of my content.

One morning the happy mother heard a voice that came from the crib. She looked, and saw a dove that played around the awakened infant. She ran to seize it. The dove did not fly away, but vanished in an instant at the very place where it had just appeared.†

---

* St. Thomas de Villanova, on the Angels
† Life of St. Neophyte, Boll

The mother understood that only an angel could make such a manifestation of himself, and, falling on her knees, she thanked me for the good-will I showed her child.

V.

The Little Brother.

HE was a child of God, as I was, but I was his elder brother, and the Heavenly Father had intrusted my little brother to me.*

"Thou shalt bear him the most tender affection," had He said to me; "and thou wilt find in my heart the measure of thy devotion."

I gazed upon the heart of God, and I saw there the source whence welled forth the Creation, the Incarnation, the Redemption, the Blessed Eucharist.†

* Marchant, Jardin des Pasteurs.
† S. Bernard, Sermon on St. Michael. Pierre de Blois, Sermon on St. Michael. Louis de Blois, Retreat of a Faithful Soul.

At the sight of this measureless chain of wonders — each link of which bore the impress of infinite charity — I was overwhelmed. The clear light of glory even could not unveil to me the depth of such mysteries, and the language spoken in heaven was powerless to tell my transports.

But when, after admiring this love, I became the instrument of it, with what fire did I burn!

In bestowing by my hands, the Heavenly Father filled me with the sentiments that led Him to give. My duties made me a sharer in His tenderness, and caused me to taste its delights. I lived no longer for myself only. Henceforth there was one life in two beings. I felt urged to impart to my brother the perfections I had received.

God was working in me. He watched with my eyes, He heard with my ear, He

* St. Hilary of Poitiers, Comment on the 129th Psalm.

ran with my feet, He flew with my wings, loved with my heart.*

I was the personification of His providence, and I felt the unspeakable joy of loading with favors the little brother He had given me.*

* St. Thomas, De Angelis, q. 113, art. 5.

VI.

The Vision.

VISIBLE to those in heaven, on earth I eluded every human eye. Like the adorable Providence I represented, I only made known my presence by my benefits.

One day, however, I made a reflection of my beauty pass before the eyes of this young soul. I did not manifest to her all my brilliancy. No one in exile could bear the full sight of an angel in glory. I borrowed sensible forms, and during sleep I allowed her to look upon me.*

* St. Ambrose, Comment. on St. Luke. Origen, Comment. on St. Luke. Life of St. Bridget, Boll.

I appeared to her with a shining countenance, with flowing hair, with a crown of flowers on my head, with a tunic of azure girt with gold, and with wings of white.*

"Wings! wings for me, too!" cried the child, in transport, and holding out its arms to me.†

Wings! was not that all it wanted to be an angel? I gave them to it in its dream. What raptures of delight! Lighter than a bird, it darted away — it flew. . . .‡

"Look!" cried the child. "I can follow my guide everywhere. Without trouble I raise myself with him above the clouds; I am going to take my seat in the bright places of heaven; I balance myself in the rays of the sun; I see the stars under my feet; immense space only is over me. The angels salute me; the blessed recognize me as one

* Life of St. Frances of Rome, Boll.
† Procopius of Gaza, Comment. on Numbers.
‡ Nicetas, Comment. on St Michael and St Gabriel.

3 *

of them; little children smile on me; Mary gives me her hand; Jesus blesses me. . . ."

All at once the babe awakes. He searches, he cries. . . . "What has become of them?"

"Be comforted, captive angel: if thou be pure, one day thy wings will be given thee; the dream will become real."

It was in this way I began to draw him toward heaven, inspiring him with love for those beautiful things the gross senses can never comprehend.*

* Theodoret, Comment on Daniel

VII.

My Co-laborers.

I WAS not alone. By the side of the infant, with me, were two valuable aids.

One had as his heritage wisdom and authority, and was distinguished for the energy of his faith. The other, by the sweetness of her look, and the goodness that showed itself in her smile, revealed the amiable piety that animated her.

Such Christian parents filled the sanctuary of infancy with the perfume of their virtue.

Their concurrence was my strength. If

they were able to do nothing without me, what could I have done without them? How many of my brothers have seen their efforts paralyzed, from having been deprived of such aid! *

Without understanding what she saw, the young soul was struck by it, and kept the memory of it. Like a spotless mirror, she reflected the pious pictures hung on the walls, the rosary in the hands of her mother, the book from which holy teaching was read, the crucifix before which prayers were said.

All the little domestic scenes were re-produced there in the light of grace, and each person left there a trace of the part he played.

To know the history of this family it was enough to see it.

Her imagination, her memory, her spirit received, from without, salutary impressions.

* St Thomas, De Angelis, q. 113, art. 4.

On arriving at the age of reason, she will be already formed to good.

Wisdom will have come before it, and, without having been sought, will have become her companion.

C

VIII.

𝕷𝖎𝖇𝖊𝖗𝖙𝖞.

IN spite of my care and of that of its parents, this child could have made shipwreck. He had received from God free-will. The crown of the elect is a gift, but it is a recompense too. The Creator gives it only to the merit of the creature. It depends on man to be good, or become wicked. If he wishes, he will be saved; if he is lost, he has willed it himself.*

Limited to counsel and to persuasion, my part was a source of the most delightful emotions, as well as of the most poignant anxiety.

* St. Thomas of Villanova, Sermon on the Glory of Heaven.

The spirit that leads a world through space admires its docility. How greatly was I compelled to admire that of an intelligent soul! The first time that she turned to God under my influence, I was filled with joy. But the fear of resistance to my voice was to me not without bitterness.

This harp, just now tuned by my hands to give forth accents of innocence, of humility, of charity, may to-morrow by caprice give herself over to Satan, and utter gross sounds of luxury, of pride, of envy, and of all the criminal passions.

I was like a mother who would see her child on the brink of a precipice. She calls, she cries out, she entreats. On his part a wicked heart urges the imprudent one to close his eyes, to take one step more. . . . Which voice will the child heed? Alas, who could tell? He is free.*

O Liberty! who, then, of angels or of

* Peter of Poitiers, Sentences, lib. ii.

men, will dare look on thee without fear? Thou art truly the tree of life and of death; thou bearest the fruits of salvation and of perdition. Gathered with discernment, they give the joys of immortality; plucked at hazard, they cause grief without end. To thee are due the delights of heaven; from thee have come the horrors of hell!

IX.

The Sanctuary.

OT only could the child resist my influence, but it could also take from me the sight of its heart.*

'T is a privilege given to man as well as to the angel to be master of himself, and to have a power over his interior feelings that no creature can share.

God only can, without their consent, penetrate the secrets of the angelic and of the human heart.

As a lily opens under the rays of the

* St. Thomas, De Angelis, q. 57, art 4. Bail., Théol Affect. des Anges.

sun, the young soul had unfolded herself to my eye, and had revealed what was hidden from others. I saw there thoughts arise, judgments formed, the affections grow, intentions directed to their aim.

One day every thing vanished from my sight. By an unfortunate impulse, the soul closed upon herself, veiled her beauty, and hid from me her treasures.

A strange breath had passed over the flower, and the flower had shut up its chalice. Great was my distress! How could I, without the inward view of this soul, cultivate in her good feelings and holy thoughts?—fight against evil thoughts and feelings?

But this state did not last long.

Simplicity and candor opened the sanctuary to me anew, and I came back to discharge there my sweet duties.

Without hindrance I could contemplate the glory of my lily, and bring to it its drop of dew.

X.

The First Fruits.

ON its knees, its hands joined, looking toward heaven, the child said, "Jesus! Mary!" Just as a flower, on opening when the morning dawns, breathes forth its first perfume, so the innocent soul sent up her first prayer to God.

He who presides over the harmony of worlds and gives enchantment to the melody of our music, bent forward and gave ear. No chord seemed to have for him a charm like that of this infant voice.

Strengthened by faith, the reason of the child began to discern between good and evil.

Fearing to offend a God so good, whom he saw served with love by his father and mother, he kept from the evil that would have flattered his passions, and did the good that cost him effort.

This sacrifice was nothing in the eyes of men; but offered on the immaculate altar of a young heart, the first act of virtue was accepted as a victim of great price.

What emotions did I experience! what hopes I conceived!

This first flower told of a delightful spring; in the first grains I saw a splendid harvest; to this beautiful dawn a most beautiful future was to succeed.

The seed I had intrusted to the soil had not perished; it had put forth its shoot, and had just blossomed.

This spectacle made me redouble my vigilance; it had excited the jealousy of Satan. Satan, too, wished to have his first fruits.

XI.

𝔗𝔥𝔢 𝔖𝔢𝔯𝔭𝔢𝔫𝔱.

THE infernal serpent succeeded in gliding into the paradise of innocence, and all at once was seen among the children of God.* He had not only borrowed from man his voice: he had taken also his countenance, bearing, and exterior. He had become incarnate in a vicious young man, and it was that moved the young man's tongue, eyes, and hands.† Under the mask of this instrument no one could detect him. He ap-

---

* Job i. 6.　　　† Tertullian, De Spectaculis.

proached without exciting distrust, and came to play with his victim.

To taint a soul so pure, to tear from God a heart so devoted to him — what a triumph!

The child looked smilingly at the sword, caressed the hand of the murderer, bent over the abyss, ran every risk.

Where was I then? At his side, I redoubled my care; I spread my wings before his eyes, and I protected him with an invisible cuirass.

He was safe. The tooth of the tawny beast had but touched the fleece of my little lamb. The cruel wolf had to fly without having glutted his rage.

But during this scene the sight of the Divine Face had enkindled my zeal; my anger was roused; my indignation burst forth.

Against the corrupter I lanced the malediction with which each guardian angel is armed by God, the friend and protector of infancy.†

*St Thomas of Villanova, On the Angels. John Lopez, Abridg ment of the Doctrine of the Fathers

† St. Matt. xviii 6, 10.

XII.

Accidents.

MY little brother was running there upon the lawn; I was with him, and followed each one of his movements.*

An insect, that had sucked from the juice of plants a subtle poison, came flying about him. The child tried to catch it, to seize it. . . . With a breath I chased away the insect, and saved my brother.

Over the grass a venomous serpent was gliding. With its eye on fire, darting forth its forked tongue, it was about to spring. With

*J. Marchant, Jardin des Pasteurs. Life of St. Bridget, Boll.

the tip of my wing I made a beautiful but-
terfly leave the bosom of a rose. The child
took to following it: the reptile was avoided.

These almost daily accidents were not the
only ones in which I was obliged to interfere.
There were others that required a visible
aid.*

The angel of death had just touched the
brow of the child with his sceptre: a deathly
pallor and motionless members told that life
was departing.

The parents at once turn to me: shall I
not be able to give back to them him who
was their happiness, and who should be the
prop of their old age, the light of their eyes,
the joy of their fireside?

If his virtue were hereafter only to make
sad shipwreck, 'mid the rocks of this world,
I should prefer seeing him, at this moment,
called, and safe in port.

* St Thomas, De Angelis, q. 113, art. 6. St. Anthony of Padua,
Sermons

But the watchfulness and counsels of a father and of a mother, penetrated with a sense of their duty, made me argue better of him, and I besought the Heavenly Physician to deign to hear their vows. My prayer had its wished-for acceptance. From the celestial heights Raphael was sent, the comforter of the sick and the weak.

The archangel came to me, and gave me the remedy, and said to me: "It belongs to thee to apply it, but to God to give it efficacy." *

I bent over the child; I traced on his brow the cross. . . . He was healed!

On waking as from a deep sleep, he cast around him a look of astonishment: "Why," he asked, "these cries, and these tears." †

What thanksgiving on the part of the parents! But neither Raphael nor I could take to ourselves the honor of such a favor.

* Origen, Comment on Jeremiah li
† Lives of St. Thyrsus, of St. Cuthbert, of St. Udalric, Boll

Only to God, whom we serve, be the honor and the glory! From Him alone flows all the good that comes to man, through the ministry of the angels.*

* Tobias xii. 6.

XIII.

The Lesson.

I LED him to the priest, who was giving, in the temple, instruction to youth.*

The good pastor was seen surrounded by little children. The affection he showed them brought to my mind that of the Saviour. He knew all intimately, he called them by name, and treated them with respect. He saw in them the infant Jesus, and used, in correcting their faults, the zeal and delicacy he would have shown in assuaging their sorrows.†

* St. Gregory Thaumat., Eulogium of Origen.
† Lives of St. Lactinus, St. Infant, and of St. M. Magdalen de' Pazzi, Boll.

47

"Dear little children," he would say to them, "I give myself all to you, to teach you to know and to bless God; but ask first your guardian angels to obtain me light and love."

The children offered with joy a prayer, that a heart full of sweetness dictated them. We accepted it at once, and like doves, we mounted to heaven, whence we brought precious graces. The humble catechist thus made our presence at his lessons useful.

From the beginning to the end my goodwill was shared between the master and pupil. The master captivated me by the skill with which he brought down to the capacity of a child treasures gathered by long study. The disciple touched me in receiving with open trustfulness the highest mysteries. I was not idle. I seconded the zeal of the priest, and his pupil was always mine. I chased away the mists from the mind of the child, and gave his understanding more clearness and extent. I gave truth brighter colors, and made more transparent the veils through which its light came. I placed in relief the beauties of faith, the charms of virtue, the magnificence of religion. I ceased not from fighting against sloth, the perfidious demon that kills in their germ the richest qualities and the purest talent.*

With such aid, fervor had advanced with knowledge, and the heart had acquired the admirable sensibility a lively faith gives.

One day his feelings could not be restrained. A pious voice was telling of the sufferings and death of the Redeemer. The child felt his soul rent with grief, and a tear moistened his eyelid. How beautiful he seemed to me! how touching was his look! More than one seraphim in his heavenly country envied this tear of a child in exile.

---

* St Nilus, On Prayer. St Sophronius, On the Angels. St Denis, On the Celestial Hierarchy. St Bernard, Comment. on Canticle of Canticles. Evagrius of Pont. Euxin, Letter to Anatolius. Life of St Andrew Salus, Boll

XIV.

The Preparations.

ITH his longings he bade the beautiful day come. Like him, I awaited its coming with impatience. From the eve, angels and children were together at the foot of the altar. The souls of the future communicants had just been purified. The imperfections that remained were thrown into the bosom of mercy or disappeared like straws in the furnace.

A God was to be received: it was a heaven that we had wished to prepare. In those souls we had made shine the precious stones of faith, of charity, of modesty, of humility, of devotedness.* We contemplated their beauty, and we showed to each other the crowns we held over their heads. Our own did not seem to us to shed a sweeter perfume.

My pupil passed the day under the influence of a smiling dream with which I had favored him during the night.

In the midst of the open heavens I had shown him the Son of God, carrying His Body, under the form of food, and presenting It to the Angels. The angels immediately hastened to Him, and prepared to receive It. With a sign He motioned them away, and, pointing out to them, on earth, the children grouped around the Sacred Table, said, "There are my guests!" "Happy children!" cried the angels.

By this picture I had given him an idea of the goodness and condescension of God toward him.

* St. J. Chrysostom, Sermon 21   Odo of Cluny, Comment. on Job.

XV.

A Shadow Dispelled.

ONE angel had remained silent and sorrowful: his hand carried no crown. He said to us, weeping:

"Happy angels, your portion is joy; your brother's, grief! Yet a few hours, and the soul that God has intrusted to me will be covered with profaned blood, and will have in reserve for her only anathemas. Sin is in her heart, and with sin the bonds, the reed, the scourges, the thorns, the cross, the nails, the lance, death!" *

We joined our prayers with those of the

* Pierre le Chantre, Verbum Abbreviatum, 30.

angel : no effect. In the midst of the light that flooded us there was that sinister shadow.

A thought came to me I gave the child I loved above all, a secret presentiment of what he did not know. Under the stimulus of grace he became recollected. His countenance expressed alarm. I suggested to him these words :

"No, my God, 1 will never betray thee. I am firmly convinced of this. But this frightful misfortune! ah, if it were to happen to one of my companions. . . . I conjure Thee, O Sovereign Master of hearts, work a miracle of thy mercy, rather than permit any one of us to give Thee into the power of the devil and crucify Thee!"*

While our Lord was receiving this prayer, a crown fell from heaven into the hands of the angel in tears.

The young sinner had risen; he had trampled under foot false shame; his fault

---

* Life of St. Mary Magdalen de' Pazzi, Boll

5 *

had been remitted. All hearts were pure, all countenances serene.*

But two angels seemed more joyful than the rest, and felt themselves mutually drawn toward each other by the liveliest sympathy: the angel of the child that had been converted, and the angel of the child that had prayed.

* Life of St. Paul the Simple, Boll.

XVI.

The Joyful Day.

WHEN he awoke, his heart bounded within him. Is this the dawn of the day of joy? So often has it been the object of my impatience! Is it not a new illusion?*

Bending over him, I said as Gabriel to Mary: "Hail! child full of grace, to-day thy Lord is going to be with thee, and thou shalt be blessed among all children."

With a joyous expanse of heart, he said to me: " Be it done unto me according to thy

* Life of St. Mary Magd. de' Pazzi.

55

word, O my good angel! and may the will of God be accomplished in me."

Two festive bands set out to meet each other.

On the part of the earth came the young child. To present him to his Lord he had not only his angel, but his father, his mother, his brothers, his friends, his teachers, the confidant of his first frailties, the whole Church. All were happy to see him admitted among the guests of Jesus Christ.*

From heaven came down the God of youth, accompanied by the angels. The inhabitants of that country of us all could not sufficiently admire his condescension. What they possessed and saw unveiled in the bosom of glory, was about to bestow itself on an obscure child.†

On one side and on the other there were lights, incense, and music.

---

* Life of St Colomba of Rieti, of St. Luthgarde, Boll.

† St James of Jerusalem, The Holy Mass Lives of SS Angela, Veronica, Cath. of Siena, Boll.

At the approach of Jesus I ran to prostrate myself before him. Majesty crowned His brow; grace reposed upon His lips; blessings beamed from His eye; in His hands dwelt almighty power.*

I accompanied Him to the throne that awaited Him. "All here belongs to Thee, Lord! this body and this soul, these faculties and these senses shall be employed only for Thy service, and in this sanctuary only Thy love shall reign."

I took these resolutions, with which I had inspired my brother, and presented them to the Guest of his heart. Jesus answered me:

"Thou, thyself, O my faithful servant, shalt watch over these treasures, and guard them from the evil spirit."

Among the angels there arose a holy envy: to repose on the bosom of Jesus, like the well-beloved disciple; to receive Jesus in his body, and have him dwell in his soul; what

* Life of St Angela

touching familiarity! what intimate union!
To which of the pure spirits was there ever
granted anything like this? *

The child was in the midst of these magnificent realities: he knew it: he was penetrated with it; but he saw them only through
the shadow of faith. He was like a blind
man walking through a garden of delight,
culling there the Divine fruit, tasting its
sweetness, but unable to contemplate its
beauty.

* Philip the Solitary, Letter to the Monk Callirus.

XVII.

The Bearer of Christ.

FROM this instant my affection for the young man was joined with the greatest respect. A God dwelt in him: it was the bearer of Christ whom I had to lead.*

The God of the Eucharist had taken possession of his soul to guide her growing powers; He made her live of His life, that He might crown her with His virtues.

When a choice bud has been engrafted on a wild trunk, the tree soon sends upward

* St. Cyril of Jerusalem, Catecheses, 4.

toward heaven fruitful branches, and beholds with astonishment this new foliage, and this fruit not its own.

So the soul, through her union with Jesus, became enriched with merits foreign to her nature, which, by her unaided powers, she never could have acquired. One would say it was a heavenly growth acclimated on earth, and flourishing there by a superior virtue.

But at the same time that my respect for the young man had increased, my fear in presence of the Divine Majesty had diminished.

Softened by the eucharistic veils, the adorable light had become accessible to my look, and I was the less dazzled by it the closer I considered it.

My relations with the God made Man were direct and constant. My duties had gained me the privilege of an ineffable intimacy. In their discharge rights were granted me to which the noblest of creatures would not of itself have dared pretend.

XVIII.

Presentation to Mary.

EHOLD, O Blessed Mother, thy child; behold him singing, like thee, his magnificat, for the God who putteth down the haughty and raiseth up the humble has just cast upon him His glance."

The reception was full of the outpouring of love. Without being seen, Mary drew him to her, and honored him with her caresses.*

"It was thus," said she, "that Jesus was sweet and modest, affectionate and confiding.

* Life of St. Angela, Boll.

These are His eyes, His features, His bearing. Jesus himself is before me. My two sons are but one, through the sacrament of love."

Pressing around us, the angels exclaimed to each other in admiration:

"What resemblance to the Divine Youth of Judea! Would it not be said that Jesus is between Mary and Joseph? The same innocence, the same docility, the same devotion!"

The child said to Mary:

"Every day, O my Mother! this prince of Thy court, whom Thou have given me for my guide, will offer you my prayers, and will load me with Thy favors. Led by him, I will brave the tribulations of this earth, and shall reach the repose of heaven, the common meeting-place of Thy children."

No word human or angelic could tell the impressions I had while I was the means of communion between these two hearts. Through me communed mother and child,

my sovereign and my brother, glory and
obscurity, home and exile.

Placed at the point of contact between two
worlds, one hand raised toward the most beloved creature of heaven, the other given to
him I loved best on earth, I was the perpetual echo of maternal tenderness and filial
piety.   Through my heart sighs went up,
and blessings descended.

XIX.

Native Air.

E went to those founts that send throughout the earth life drawn from heaven.

"See," said I, "thy true country. 'T is there thou wert born to grace, and wert adopted by that family of which God is the Father, Mary the mother, Jesus the eldest son, Christians the children, Angels the ministers.*

He renewed his protestations of fidelity to Jesus, his renouncement of the world, his anathemas against Satan.

The water of his baptism had been reli-

* St. Leo, Serm. 5 on the Nativity.

giously preserved. It was placed before him. He kissed with grateful love the vase that held it, and wished to have a drop placed on his brow.*

In these pious transports he breathed forth from his heart these words I suggested to him:

"Dear waters, you grow large before my eyes, and take the proportions of a vast river.

"You recall the wonders more touching to me than those the Jordan saw, and you are yourself my Jordan, my well-beloved river.

"You saw miracles greater than the passage of the Red Sea by Moses, and were the tomb of an enemy deadlier than Pharaoh.

"It was in your bosom I found the way to the land of promise, and I owe it to you that I dwell in it to-day, to quench my thirst at refreshing springs, to purify myself in limpid streams, to breathe saving perfumes, to cull the fruits of life.

"Happy day of my baptism, I shall never

* Custom of some Christian families

6 *   E

forget thee! Sweet country, I will come often in thought to tread thy blessed soil, and seek in my native air the support of my strength. Heavenly laver, receive anew my soul, and penetrate it with thy Divine salt.

"Generous Liberator, on the scene of Thy benefits, only one favor more I ask, that of being all my life worthy of Thee."

XX.

The Buckler.

TO preserve the nobility of his soul and defend the honor of his God, the young man was to have many rude assaults to sustain. Foreseeing this, the Church wished to early arm the soldier of Christ. A new sacrament, Confirmation, wrought this consecration to heaven.

The imposition of hands, the sign of the cross, oil, balsam, a few words were what struck the senses and appeared without. But within and under the material symbols, what phenomena and what realities ! *

*Tertullian, Tract. de Resurrectione, 8.

On the forehead of the young man was stamped a character destined to proclaim his rights and recall his engagements. It was like a radiant star, the brightness of which could be dimmed, but could not be extinguished. Brave or cowardly, faithful or traitorous, for his glory or for his shame, the young soldier will bear this mark forever.

Seven mysterious elements composed the armor with which he was covered. Each was a special gift of God, and had a distinct name. They were called Wisdom, Understanding, Counsel, Fortitude, Knowledge, Piety, and Fear.

They were united and blended together by the action of the Holy Ghost, who dwelt in them, and made them resplendent.

Such an armor brought with it victory. Neither arrow nor sword could make any impression on it.

Henceforth, to triumph, the soldier had only to will it. He could await with a firm foot the most redoubtable antagonists. At his wish he would find skill for the contest, courage for the combat, heroism in the melee of battle.

Encased in his buckler, with a heart full of Divine fire, he was a terror to demons, and seemed to them like the Archangel Michael. The rays that darted from his brow wounded their eyes and compelled them to withdraw.

Let him watch, however, let him be on his guard ; let him never leave bare that breast, to-day so well protected. His implacable enemy, counting on a favorable day, sharpens his sword and his darts.

XXI.

The Infernal Lion.

IGHT and day I heard the lion roar, and I saw him prowling about us, with a rage nothing could appease. He scented a prey whose presence did not cease to excite in him a thirst for blood.*

The angels of David, of Archelaus, of Enthymius, of Martin, of Emilian, of Clement of Ancyra, gave to savage beasts the gentleness of lambs. The infernal beast alone never laid aside his ferocity.†

Wounded by the hunter, the panther turns

---

* St. Germanus of Constantinople, Sermon on the Burial of our Lord.
† Lives of several Saints, Bollandists.

with bloodshot eye, and seeks its enemy. If it cannot seize him, it springs upon anything that bears the slightest resemblance to him, and tears it to pieces.

So does also the devil. Pierced by an arrow he cannot draw out, and seeing the Divine Hunter beyond his reach, he circles round him with a threatening look.*

Living images of God —souls astray upon the earth, tremble!

The devil enjoys the ill caused to man, as if it were done to God. In dethroning God from a heart, it seems to him that he has banished Him from heaven.

To gain a soul of which he was in search, Satan would willingly have given up a host of other victims. It seemed to him that this one would have brought him a much greater number of them. Vice would have found, in the charms of a disposition by nature good, a powerful means of propagating itself.

* Gennadius, Fragments on Genesis.

And if the traitor had succeeded in making this captive an instrument of death, with what torments would he not have recompensed this complacency! To outrage God and torture souls is the aim from which the hatred of Satan never swerves.

At his approach I felt the hand of the young man clasp mine more strongly, and I heard him say, "Save me, I perish!" *

He did not perish, for he feared. His fear, mingled with confidence, kept him under my wings, and was his safety.

* St. Bernard, Comm. on Ps. xc.

XXII.

The Angel of Darkness.

SKILLED in dissimulation, the malignant spirit did not attack with open force whom he wished to destroy; he was satisfied with laying snares for him. The angel of darkness transformed himself into an angel of light.*

How often would the young man have allowed himself to be deceived, had I not aided him to foil the treachery of the Evil One! †

One night, Satan appeared to him accom-

*2d Epistle to the Corinthians xi. 14. Raoul Ardent, On the Holy Angels. St. Chrysostom, Comm. on St. Matt.

† St. Pantales, Discourse on St. Michael. Raoul Ardent, On the Holy Angels.

panied by spirits that surrounded a shining chariot.

"See this chariot of fire," said the tempter; "it is that which brought Elias up to heaven. I come to take you as I took him. You are so virtuous that the Apostles, Martyrs, Prophets, Angels, Mary herself, long to have you in their company, and enjoy your presence. Yield to their wishes; mount, and we go."

The youth had risen, he had approached the fiery car; he was about to place his foot upon it. . . . "A sign of the cross," said his angel to him. At this sacred symbol the illusion vanished, and he saw only the abyss into which he would inevitably have fallen.*

He promised thenceforward to distrust all flattering speech, and this cautious conduct was his best safeguard.

Every time he was addressed with praises

* Life of St. Simon Stylites, by St Anthony   Life of St John the Hermit, by Palladius

of his piety or of his talents, a cloud of demons flew about him, impatient to see him take pleasure in it. I would take him then in my arms, cover him with my wings, and snatch him from the peril he was in.*

Thanks to the confidence he showed me, he was able to avoid the stone in his path, escape the arrows that flew in the night, tread upon the asp and the basilisk, join me in my triumph over Lucifer, and overthrow the Apostate.†

* Life of St Macarius of Egypt, by Bollandists.
† 90th Psalm, and Commentaries on it

XXIII.

Victories.

E was already bearing aloft his banner against the spirit that had deserted his Master. Upon it was seen the chief of the heavenly hosts striking the dragon to the earth, and on it were read in flaming characters the words : " Who is like unto God ? "

Under the shadow of this banner, or rather in the light of it, not one victory only, but many victories were gained every day.

Victory in the respect for the name of God, in the face of the countless array of blasphemers ; victory in the flight from impure vice, in the midst of so many depraved hearts; victory in the contempt of seductive scandal, despite perpetual solicitations; victory in faithfulness to duty when unfaithfulness seemed to have become a title to glory.

At each victory thus obtained, in the name of the immortal King of Ages, and in His presence, I placed on the breast of the obscure hero a new mark of honor. Men did not see it, but angels admired it, and bade him be happy in the possession of it.

O noble breast! which covered itself with unspotted honor, and drew down the approving look of God! *

Between God and the devil there existed a contest with regard to this young man: who was to win his homage? who was to have his services?

Glory to God! Confusion to the devil!

* St. Isidore Pelusiota, Letter to Dorotheus the Scholastic.

7 *

Up to this time such had been the fruit of his devotion.

He was going from triumph to triumph, and was becoming rich in shining merit. Satan furnished him continual occasions for it, and gathered, without willing it, flowers for his crown.

Exercise kept him from being enervated. In action he showed more manly traits, and the image of God stamped itself on his soul in deeper lines.*

The prism under the eye of man divides the ray of light, and makes the colors of the rainbow burst forth. Just so struggle and trial, finding in a heart piety thus far uniform, made it give birth to the variety of Christian virtues. A more beautiful holiness, fruit of effort and combat, had taken the place of the infused and purely passive sanctity of his earlier days.

* St. John Chrysostom, Comm on St Matthew St Peter Damian, Opusc 23

How much did the Evil One suffer at thy sight? He only could tell. Simplicity tortured him, humility crushed him, charity crucified him.*

* St Bernard, Serm. on Dedication.

XXIV.

𝔉𝔦𝔡𝔢𝔩𝔦𝔱𝔶.

HOW beautiful were those days of innocence and of fervor! Everything in them breathed candor and purity, confidence and love. Fatherly tenderness on the one side, and filial piety on the other, held each other in perpetual embrace. No fault had changed these delightful relations.

When the father bent over his son, his look showed no trace of discontent or reproach. When the child threw himself on the bosom of his father, it was with entire self-abandonment. His fear had nothing servile in it: it came from love, and was but an exquisite delicacy. The freedom of heart with which after some forgetfulness he ran to ask pardon, gave him a new charm. His father knew his frailty; he never lost sight of the indulgence of his father.

Oh, how sweet is it to protect him who has never yet disobeyed! The guidance of this innocent soul brought me each moment new joys. I had my share in the complacency of which he was the object. The Divine Master, in contemplating him, seemed to say to me:

"It is well! I recognize in these perfections the devotion of my minister. Thou representest me worthily with my child, and thou knowest how to have for him the tenderness of a father. I could not better bestow my confidence, and I give myself praise for having placed my treasure in thy hands.

"The memory of thy mission shall not be absorbed in the delights of heaven; it shall

F

live in glory, and the splendor thou preparest for this soul, reflected on thee, shalt announce that thou wert his protector in time, as thou shalt be his friend for eternity. Thou shalt have the signal honor of having partaken with the Son of God made Man in the work of his salvation." *

But these beautiful days, which it seemed never ought to have ended, passed away, alas! with frightful rapidity, and the firmament, until then bright, was covered with dark clouds.

* St. Thomas, De Angelis, q. 113, art. 4.   St. Thomas of Villanova, On the Angels.

XXV.

Weakness.

SATAN seemed to ask so little, and his voice was so honeyed that the young man ended by listening to him. He did not commit any mortal sin, but he relaxed his fervor and lost his first charity.*

I could not tell how much this weakness saddened me; I saw in it the germ of countless failings.†

The young man no longer responded so perfectly to my care. He was insensible to my inspirations, and neglected the grace I

* Apocalypse, ii. 4
† St. Andrew of Cæsarea, Comm. on Apoc.

83

obtained for him. Vanity ruined whatever was best in him, and presumption made everything dangerous.

How could I engage that indocile spirit in prayer? How make that unmortified heart love virtue? Frivolity alone pleased his indolence; he had no taste but for low things. Every Christian thought oppressed him. The perfumes of Jesus Christ no longer had any charm for him.*

Evil everywhere took the place of good. Venial faults accumulated; those of doubtful gravity no longer caused alarm; crime insensibly lost the horror with which it inspires delicate souls.

No good desire came to perfection; no saving work was done.†

There were great merits in this soul: what was to become of them?

Are we to see a barbarous enemy devastate

* St. Andrew of Cæsarea, Comm. on Apoc.
† St. John Climacus, The Ladder of Heaven.

a land cultivated with so much love, ravage a harvest so rich, carry away the fruit of such toilsome labors?

Behold what infidelity to grace, and contempt of God's loving preference!

My first sorrows were the first joys of Satan.*

* St. Nilus, Letter to the Bishop Aristobulus.

8

XXVI.

The Threat.

THE tree now converted the precious sap only into vain foliage without fruit. It was barren in the midst of fertile soil. A curse could not fail to fall upon it. I saw the axe raised, the furnace kindled.*

I asked pardon; I supplicated, conjured, and promised more perfect culture.

A respite was granted to my urgent demands. What did I not do to turn it to account? What striving! what efforts.†

---

* St. Luke iii. 9.
† St. Pantales, Serm. on St. Michael.

On the part of the young man I met with only distraction and levity, effeminacy and disgust. I held out to him my hand, he thrust it aside; I showed him the path, he turned from it; I called him, he fled.*

Ah! had it only been given me to open his eyes, could he have failed to shudder? A black cloud, bearing the lightning above his head, was growing larger, and, under his feet, a vast abyss was opening. But he was obstinate in hearing nothing, in seeing nothing.

The Divine Master, irritated by this con- . tempt of His favors, every day became less prodigal of them; He was on the eve of carrying out one of His most terrible threats; His heart was troubled within Him; He was about to cast forth from His mouth the luke-warm servant.†

The young man dreaded the urgings of

* Jean Lopes, Abridgment of the Teaching of the Fathers.
† Apocalypse iii 16

my love, and sought to escape from them; the more ardent my zeal became, the more it excited his disgust.

I was to protect him in the ways in which God called him, but not to sustain him among all the precipices on which he might choose to venture. His presumptuous rashness kept my succor at a distance, and made my interference illusory.*

And Satan, following his purpose, made use of patience nothing could ruffle. As yet he did nothing excessive. He did not wish to offer open violence to a conscience that would have protested; he knew how, in lulling it to insensibility, to make ready his fatal blow.

* St. Bernard, Comm on the 90th Ps

XXVII.

𝔗𝔥𝔢 𝔉𝔞𝔩𝔩.

EVERYTHING had conspired to bring about the fall; and it came. I heard a voice of hell cry arrogantly: "Hence, God of Heaven! — God of Calvary and of the Cross, hence!" *

"No," said Satan, "I did not create this soul; I did not purchase her; I never took a body for her; I did not for her undergo humiliation, suffer pain.

"No one ever saw me, that I might gain her love, give my hands to be tied, present my cheek to be buffeted, shed my blood, feel

* St. Ambrose.

the horrors of agony, go down to the tomb.*

"I never offered her a heaven, nor a crown, nor a throne.

"I have done her only harm; I wish only her ruin; I have in reserve for her only torments.

"She gives herself to me, however; she chooses me for her master; she has just preferred me to her sovereign benefactor.†

"Triumph then, O my hate! She is in my power, this soul that God cherished.

"Ah! if the fire that devours me could be extinguished, it would be so by the torrent of tears I will make her shed one day.

"But the tears shed during life are often sad ones to me. Let us know how to wait those that come after death. Let us content ourselves now with blinding the victim."

Such impudent language did Satan address

---

* St Cyprian, On Good Works and Almsgiving.
† Idem.

to the accomplices of his fury; but for the soul he had only words of felicitation, the bitter irony of which she knew not how to perceive.

The book of life was open, and the incorruptible Judge had cancelled a name! . . .

Not to die of grief, at such a sight, one must be immortal, as I was.

Around me numberless voices had in affright exclaimed: "Let us fly! let us fly! let us go hence!"*

As smoke dissipates a swarm of bees, and as infection disperses a flock of pure doves, just so the odor of sin had put to flight the happy spirits.†

I alone, despite my repugnance, had remained there watching and praying.

* Flavius Josephus, The Jewish War
† St Peter Damian, Opusc 23, Life of the Ven. Widow Gentitis, Boll

XXVIII.

Tears.

HANGING over the abyss, the sinner was held back only by the very frail thread of life. He slept in time, at the risk of awaking in eternal fire.

Never had the sadness of the prophets equalled my sadness; their tears had never the bitterness of my tears.

"But just now so united, shall we be forever separated? will he, who ought to be a companion, prove only a cowardly deserter? after having been his protector and his guide, must I needs be his accuser and his judge? instead of making him a partner of my hap-

92

piness, must I ask of him an account of the love I bore him? Shall I recall to him my good deeds, only to reproach him with his ingratitude? *

"Satan my vanquisher! He whom I cast to the earth the day of his revolt, and whom since I have so often humbled! He would gain a decisive victory, and would vaunt himself of this late triumph! . . .

" The angels I see each day mounting to heaven after the judgment of the damned, are bathed in tears. They have been obliged to abandon to the devils bodies and souls: double rejoicing for hell ! †

" We wished to save them, they said, and they refused to be saved. Let us leave them in the darkness of their damnation, and celebrate the reign of justice there where the acts of Divine mercy have been rejected:

---

* Origen, Comm. on Numbers. St Augustine, Contra Julianum
† St Antoninus, Summa Theol , p iii Life of St. Andrew Salus,
Boll

Thou art just, O God! and righteous are Thy judgments.*

"Will there come a time when I shall be obliged to use such language, at once severe and full of desolation?

"Go then, thou guide that didst excite the envy of thy brethren! Show the crown woven by thy hands; count the treasures heaped up by thy zeal; proclaim incomparable the child thou hadst the honor to lead; plan beautiful projects for the future!

"Enchanting pictures, rich perspectives, magnificent hopes, all vanished like a dream!"

'T was thus my grief vented itself!

* Jeremiah li. 9, and Comm. Tobias in. 2.

XXIX.

The Chains of the Captive.

PRIDE and shame, boldness and fear, force and weakness, all were of use to the devil; everything became an obstacle in his hands to bar the return to God.

Faculties and talents had abandoned the law of the master and obeyed the usurper.

The pious impressions of the memory had become weakened, and gave place to bad recollections; the pictures of the imagination were no longer animated save by the impure spirit; the intellect saw shadows float across its beautiful rays, and the heart accustomed to noble aspirations began to seek the pleasures of earth.*

Since he had had his wings mutilated, the eagle was learning to do without pure air and sunlight. Instead taking anew his noble flight, he wallowed in the mire.

A slave, this soul did nothing for herself. She thought, meditated, planned. . . . For whom was the fruit of so much forethought, and fatigue? For a vile tyrant to whom she had surrendered herself.†

When, in the midst of this degradation, remorse made itself felt, the demon soon reassured the guilty one: " You are quick in taking alarm. Despise these vain scruples. Your conscience would become your executioner. What great evil is it to break a law that contradicts one's dearest yearnings?

* St. Augustine, Book of Questions, quest. 23. Procopius of Gaza, Comm. on Exodus

† St. Ambrose, Comm. Ps. cxviii. Procopius of Gaza, Comm. on Isaiah.

Can precepts so annoying merit such respect?"

Availing himself of one only fault, Satan wished to shatter, in this soul, the edifice of faith, and make her doubt of doctrines and of duties. He strove to bring her to that depth of evil to which the impious, when they contemn everything, have come.* Notwithstanding what I had under my eyes, I could not despair. I saw the mirror, formerly so pure, tarnished and soiled, but it was not broken. A miracle could give it back its brightness, and make it reflect again the Divine image.

* Proverbs, xviii. 3.

XXX.

Recourse to Heaven.

CALLED the angels of heaven to my aid, and conjured them to unite with me : *

"Angels of holy penitents, lend to your brother the voice that appeased the anger of God, the accent that touched His heart.

"Angel of Augustine, thou knewest this sadness; thou didst groan under these sorrows; take pity on my suffering, and fly to my aid.

"Angel who didst deliver Peter from his prison, come, break these chains more cruel

* Origen, Homily on Ezechiel.

still: the apostle was a captive of Jesus
Christ, the sinner is a slave of Satan.

"Angel who didst overthrow Saul the per-
secutor on the way to Damascus, wilt thou
not be able to cast trembling and submissive
at the feet of God this heart so rebellious to
the goad?

"Angel who didst save Lot from an
accursed place of abode, snatch this soul from
sin: sin is threatened with a fire more terrible than that of Sodom.

"Angel guardians of virtuous friends
who deplore his conduct, invite them to
pray for the unhappy young man: is not
zeal the crown of true love?

"Angels of the family, unite your efforts
to bring back to God him who grew up in
the midst of you, lived in your society,
learned lessons of you, was loaded with your
gifts, and became your sweetest joy.

"Blessed, chosen one, who wert given
him as a patron, thou art not made to be

at his side, as I am; but from the bosom of glory follow him with a look; thou wert the depositary of precious graces: here is the moment to bestow them.

"Sweet Mary, in what a condition does thy child appear to thee! Ah! in spite of his evil deeds he belongs to thee. Sinners are all thine. Refuge of sinners, pray for him!

"Saviour of souls, in the name of Thy blood that flowed without fruit, in the name of innocence, the memory of which is yet fresh, touch this soul and save her." *

* Life of St. Andrew Salus, Boll

XXXI.

The Voice of Creatures.

WITH the irresistible desire I
had for his conversion, I
could have moved heaven
and earth to work it out. Ex-
ternal objects, inanimate beings,
the most simple phenomena took a
voice and became eloquent in express-
ing to him my affectionate remonstrances.

In the midst of a storm, a voice said to
him: "This lightning is the eye of God:
this rolling thunder is the sound of His voice.
He knows thy conscience; He sees the bottom
of thy heart. If He were to call thee suddenly before His tribunal!" . . . *

At the sight of a rainbow, a voice said to him: "'T is thus the clemency of a father warns his son. Dost thou hear this sweet call? Dost thou recognize the smile of a God ready to be appeased?"

Of an evening when he happened to gaze on the azure vault and the stars, a voice said to him: "How beautiful is this heaven! how splendid! Shall it one day be thy country?"*

In the morning, when his eye ranged over the landscape, a voice said to him: "Everything sings its canticle to God; everything tells again the praises of the Most High; only the wicked heart is silent."

On seeing a cross, a voice said to him: "This ladder of Divine love, that ought to lead to the dwelling-place of the elect, thou wouldst change to an insurmountable barrier by thy obstinacy!"

At the sound of bells, a voice would say

* Life of Luther.

to him: "Is not this still a sigh for thy infidelity? When shall they ring out a peal of joy at thy return?"

A barren tree, a field covered with brambles, languishing meadows, dry sands, naked rocks, miry roads recalled to him the deplorable state of his soul.

The dew of morning, the limpid brook, the fertile rain, the refreshing breeze represented to him the varied graces made fruitless by his insensibility.

The enamel of the prairies, the richness of the harvest, the treasures of the spring, the chorus of birds, the hum of insects spoke to him words of just reproach.

On all sides, on earth and in the heavens, mysterious voices assailed his ear with these terrible words: "Ungrateful man! we are the benefits bestowed on thee by Him thou hast outraged. How long wilt thou compel us to serve a slave of the Evil One, and bend us to his caprice?"

XXXII.

The Father's Call.

GREAT was the gap the young man had placed between his father and himself. A messenger of rapid wing lessened the distance.

While the guilty one was thought abandoned, he was receiving through me continued favors. Never was I the confidant of more touching goodness, and never did I see better the tenderness there is in the heart of a father.

This incomparable feeling grew with the obstacles and the ingratitude that repaid it, and placed in higher relief its Divine traits.

It was in the name of the Heavenly Father that I went to lay before the eyes of the prodigal the smiling picture of the places whence he had fled. I represented to his imagination the tree under which, as a child, he had played, the garden that had given him its flowers, the brook that bathed the green lawns, and the roof that had covered his peaceful joys.

'T was the Heavenly Father that said, by my voice: "What day was marked by severity and rigor? what moment but brought thee new proofs of love? Must thou be reminded of the caresses, of the outpourings, of the inexhaustible indulgence for thy first infidelity? The abundance in which thou didst live, the zeal of thy servants, the devotion of thy family — dost thou complain of these? Dost thou prefer these rags, this slavery, this contempt, all these spectres of misery that rise around?

"Hasten to return. The arms of thy

father are always open to his child. Everything calls thee. See the couch on which
thou didst repose, and the rich ring destined
for thee, the gay robe, and the festive sandal
of honor, and the banquet of joy!

"That our morning gatherings have their
freshness, our meetings at eventide their delights, our reunions their life, thou only art
wanting to us. Thou only canst dry our
tears, smooth our brows, give happiness to
our hearts."

XXXIII.

The Resolve.

S O much love could not fail to touch a heart that had remained good. The youth has seen his misery; he has blushed at it; hope has held out her hand to him; he will retrace his steps.

His passions forthwith cling to him, trying to keep him back:

Thou art going to abandon us? Impossible dream! Thou wilt not be able to live without us. Thou wilt raise thyself only to fall back again. An attempt so mad will be a new occasion of greater confusion to thee.*

* St. Augustine, Confessions, l. 8, c. xi

107

Showing him then the souls of all ages and of every rank that were leading a holy life, I said to him:

"What! my brave young man, thou wilt not be able to do what these women, these virgins, these old men, and these children have been able to do? Wilt thou persist in not knowing thyself? or dost thou count on doing without aid from on high? Know that to work prodigies, grace only asks a frank and loyal co-operation." *

The companions of his faithlessness addressed him in specious words:

"Who would be willing to believe in thy sincerity? Who but will see cowardice in this step? Does thy father promise to pardon thee? Will he cease on that account to throw up to thee thy evil deeds?"

I answered:

"Know the heart of a father better, and insult him not with feigned consideration.

* St Augustine, Confessions, l 8, c xi

When he pardons, 't is without restriction. Has one single fault been known to have been cast up as a reproach to the greatest sinners? Human indulgence and mercy can be subject to disagreeable reminding; Divine pardons, never."

Grace overcame the last resistance. The child said to himself:

"How many servants in my father's house have bread in abundance, and I am perishing from hunger! I will arise, and I will go to my father, and I will say to him: Father! I have sinned against heaven and before thee; I am not worthy to be called thy son; receive me as one of thy servants.*

*St. Luke xv.

10

XXXIV.

The Return.

I LED him to the tribunal where clemency sits, where charity reigns, where the guilty man is the more sure of pardon the more severely he accuses himself.

The sinner told with sorrow the faults, of which he had asked joy, and which had given him sadness.

As he went on telling them he became consoled, and shed tears of gratitude.

An angel had moved the waters of the pool in which he had plunged. I had given the soul of the priest a zeal wholly godlike, and I had placed on his lips words that equalled in sweetness those of pure spirits.

When the minister of reconciliation stretched forth his hand and opened his mouth to pronounce sentence, infinite mercy was in his heart.

Like the God who forgave through his voice, he forgot faults that were no longer, and remembered only the condescension of a father and the generous action of a son.

While this scene was enacting in the secrecy of the tribunal, there were signs of joy at the sacred font, sighs of love in the tabernacle, marks of impatience above the holy table, mysterious voices everywhere through the sanctuary.

The angels were there to bid the sinner rejoice, to give him courage in this step, to aid him in his penance.*

* St. Thomas of Villanova, On the Angels.

XXXV.

The Feast.

THE Heavenly Father could not contain his joy. He called together his friends, told them his happiness, bade them join him in giving a beautiful reception to his son. The angels have seen Him go forward to meet his child, throw himself upon his neck, bathe him with his tears. They have heard the cry of His heart :

"Quick! fetch his robe of old, and clothe him with it; put the ring on his finger, and sandals on his feet. Bring hither the fatted calf, kill it, let us feast and rejoice, for this my son was lost, and he is found, he was dead, and he has come to life." *

The angels have obeyed; they have given back to the young man his dignity and rank. They have spread the table, they have lit the lamps, they have twined the garlands. The ministers of the sanctuary are to adorn the altar, prepare the victim, sacrifice the Divine Lamb, who wills to give himself as nourishment.

The wine of consolation flows in full stream; delicious viands are brought from halls above. 'T is no longer only a few crumbs fallen from the tables at which princes sit: 't is the universality of spiritual goods.

The Lord hath said to his eldest born:

"Complain not, O glorious spirits! if I have not happened to do thus.for every one of you. You are always with me, and all I have is yours." †

* St. Luke xv   † Ibid

" Allow a father to take unbounded pre-caution, when he is going to touch the bleed-ing wounds of his child.

" You, that never felt the bitterness of absence, nor the privations of being de-spoiled, nor the weight of slavery, nor the hardship of disgrace, remain in the posses-sion of your joy, and by your union become the interpreters between two sundered hearts that have again found each other."

At this invitation of the father of the family the heavenly musicians take their places above the festive table, and prepare to sing the delights of this day of rejoicing.*

At the conversion of one sinner they show more joy than at the perseverance of ninety-nine just.   The breath of fatherly tenderness animates the lyres, and lives in their notes.†

The angels tell successively of the power of tears, and of the triumph of love.

* St. Luke xv 25   † Ibid 7

XXXVI.

The Power of Tears.

HAIL, happy tears! hail, cause of our joy!

"You are stronger than Satan from whom you tore his victim, more powerful than hell, the chains of which you shattered.

"You raise yourself above every creature, and you dictate laws to the Almighty.

"You alone have changed justice into mercy, and made of an angry judge a father full of love.

"You have taken the place of words and of eloquence, of supplication and of prayer.

"In the eyes of a sinner you are more beautiful than the reflection of heaven in the eyes of the just.*

"In you sparkle the blood of redemption, the treasures of grace, the wonders of eternity.

"You open the heart to hope, and place on the predestined brow the sign of salvation.†

"You wash out from the guilty soul a stain that not all the united waters of rivers and of seas would have been able to take away.

"You are the dew of spring that tells of the sighs of the dove in the fields of Divine love.‡

"You are the wine that rejoices angels,

* St. J. Chrysost., Comment. Ep. ad Coloss.
† St. Augustine, Homil. 27.
‡ Hugo a St. Caro, Comment. in Cant. Canticor.

and the pure water the God of the Cross thirsts after.*

"Shed in exile, you cause in the heavenly country universal joy.

"The eternal unhappiness of the fallen angel will be never to have shed one such tear.†

"Hail, happy tears! hail, cause of our joy!"

* St. Bernard, Comment. on the Canticle of Canticles. St. Chrysostom, Sermon 93.
† St. Vincent Ferrer., Sermons.

XXXVII.

The Triumphs of Love.

DECK thee with fresh verdure, O withered meadow; bear thy smiling harvests, ravaged field! Put forth thy flower's stem, once rudely spoiled; tree left desolate and barren, bend thy branches under the weight of fruit.

"Admirable everywhere, in no place has Divine condescension revealed itself by more touching effects. It has not let live one of the faults pardoned, and it has, through penance, made lost merits live again.

"The sinner feels anew the crown of the

elect encircle his brow. He can contemplate it at even when he rests, and salute it in the morn when he wakes. He sees it floating in his dream at night, and finds it while he meditates by day.

"O prince! fallen yesterday, to-day raised up, hold with both hands thy crown of royalty, repel the hand that would tarnish it, or tear away its emblems.

"The heavenly pastor has countless flocks in the verdant pasture-grounds of grace and of glory. Thousands of sheep graze in the valleys of the earth. Still more leap and play on the lofty hills of heaven, clothed in their fleeces of pure white. All together could not have consoled him for the loss of only one. In that one he seemed to have lost all. What joyous heart-beats, when he brought her back to the fold, and she rested with her sisters, under the guardian care of the well-loved crook of her shepherd.

"Come out of your dens, monsters of the

desert! run in pursuit of the lamb. You shall never be able to quench your thirst in its blood. The tender care of the pastor has been quicker and more active than the fury of the wolves.*

"At the word of Divine friendship, the seal of the sepulchre has flown to pieces, the stone has been rolled back, the bonds have been sundered; he who had been dead four days, has arisen full of life. What a hymn these renewed senses sing! Resurrection! Word ineffable, those will never understand thy sweet mysteries who have not gone down to the tomb. Will they comprehend better the transports of the Divine friend, who receives in his arms him whose loss he had bewailed?

"O grave! where is thy victory? O death! where is thy sting? Jesus has wept over Lazarus. Oh, how much He loved him."†

* St. Luke xv
† Ep St. Paul ad Cor. I. xv 55. St John xi. 36.

XXXVIII.

A Sound Escapes from Heaven.

WHILE the angels were cele-
brating the return of the
sinner, a lament came up to
heaven.

"No," said a voice, "I can
no longer bear pains so atrocious.
Whatever may be the delights of recompense,
they cannot be in proportion to such a pun-
ishment. Hear my prayer, O compassionate
God! Make haste to comfort Thy feeble
creature."

This lament passed like a sigh through the
songs of joy, and went straight to the heart
of God. Our melodies did not keep the

Most High from hearing it, and giving answer.

As we continued our strains, He opened slightly the door that bars from men the accents of the blessed.

One sound only, the least penetrating of our melodies, escaped from our strains, and went to touch lightly this suffering heart.

"Enough! enough! or I die!" cried the servant of God. His soul had thrilled, like those of the elect, and had received a foretaste of infinite happiness. The pleasure had been so lively, that had the sound lasted one instant more, she would have burst the bonds that held her and have flown to us.*

* Life of St. Francis of Assisium.

XXXIX.

The Spiteful Rage of the Usurper.

THE song of the angels excited the spiteful rage of Satan. The envy that devours his inmost being, since the exaltation of man, showed itself more terrible, and made him give forth cries of fury.*

If he suffers at the sight of a soul he rapaciously covets and which he cannot seize, how much sharper is his pain where he loses the prey he had in his hands.†

He could not withhold the transports of

* St. Augustine, De Civ. Dei, lib. xii. c. 9.
† Life of St. Aldegunda, Boll.

his rage at the blow that had just struck him.

"Why chase me from the abode where I dwelt in peace? Why deprive me of the pleasure I had in doing harm? Could I not hope to enjoy it yet awhile? To keep me from ruining man is to make my hell a hundred-fold worse.*

"Besides, in what does this soul deserve to be preferred to me? What title can she have to be, by preference, aided by mercy, when I am given over to the rigors of justice? Is she more worthy of pardon than I am? Had she sinned less often or less mortally than I? Let them count the faults of Lucifer, and let them weigh him in the balance. Let them put side by side the iniquities of man and that slight movement of pride! . . . Man may become guilty a thousand and a thousand times; as often will he obtain pardon; after one only fault, Lucifer

* Theophylactus, Comm on St. Matthew.

shall be punished without redress.   Where in this is there justice ? " *

At these words the blessed spirits and glorified souls unite in one voice, and, with a sound like to thunder, exclaim :

" When did Satan repent him ?   When did he penance ? "

Confounded at this reproach, Satan had vanished.†

.Life of St. Eudoxia, Boll.   † Idem.

11 *

XI.

The Happy Fault.

I NEVER loved my brother more tenderly than since his glorious resuscitation, after his fall. He was more completely mine — for he owed his life to me once more. I had concurred in his baptism and in his repentance, in his birth and in his resurrection.*

His soul had become adorned with perfections she had never had in her best days of innocence: her love had in it something more generous, more lively, stronger.†

Jealous in repairing lost time, she dreamed

* Tertullian, Tr. de Pœnit., c. viii.
† St. Ambrose, On the Tears of St. Peter, Serm. 47.

126

only of the means of drawing from past evil
future good. ,

In the face of danger I suggested to her a
thousand reflections on her imprudence, and
laid before her eyes the torments she had
undergone in consequence of it.

One look was enough to bring her to herself, to make her shed tears, to secure her
fidelity.*

Having escaped, stripped of her plumage
and covered with blood from the claws of the
vulture, the dove would take refuge in the
bosom of her mother. At these times, as I
pressed her under my wings to give her new
warmth, I felt her beautiful youth come back
again.

She took such precautions against surprise
and conceived so great horror of vice, and
acquired such a taste for virtue, that I could
at length exclaim : " Happy fault ! "

* St. Augustine, Tr de Corrept. et Gratia, c i   St. J. Chrysos., s.
107.   J. Lopes, Abstract of Doctrine of H. Fathers

XLI.

The Counsellor.

TO prevent new wanderings, I inspired the young man with the thought of consulting me in everything hereafter, bringing to mind my presence, in all his actions.*

If he had been invited to a worldly assembly: "I could not go without thee, O my heavenly friend!" he said, "and I should not dare ask thee to take me thither."

If a bad book fell into his hands: "Could I direct thy look, so pure, on pages dictated by Satan?"

* St. Andrew of Cæsarea, Comm. on Apocalypse.

If he were moved to revenge: "Would not an invisible arm arrest and hold back the blow I meditate!" *

If he felt a humbling temptation: "Should I dare before a prince of heaven, what I should not venture to do before the lowest of my fellow-men?"

If he heard wicked discourses: "Could I listen to words that will wound my best friend to the heart?"

If he were in danger of scandalizing his neighbor: "This would be to join the service of the demons, and fight against the ministry of the angels!"

If he were affrighted at the difficulty of duty: "Help me, thou who art my support; I will not have thee blush for my cowardice." †

He did nothing without my approbation.

* J. Marchant, Jardin des Pasteurs.

† St. Lawrence Justinian, Tr de Disciplina Monastica, 5. St. Sophronius, On the Angels.

Everything was submitted to me. I reigned over his spirit and directed his actions. He shared my wisdom, and was led by my light.

XLII.

The Future.

TIME went on. What perspective was going to open before the youth? What was to be my ministry?

Should I have to stand one day at the side of a priest at the altar, or of a religious in the depth of the cloister, or of a soldier on the field of battle?

Nothing had revealed to me the secret of God. I saw in no present cause the events of the future; and He who knows all things, had not spoken.*

* Theodoretus, Comm. on the 24th Ps. Bail., Théol. Affect. des Anges.

I knew not into what path the young man obeying the call of heaven would lead me; I imagined myself beforehand in a variety of situations.

The priesthood was the object of my admiration and of my complacency. What a crown is reserved for the faithful dispenser of Divine graces, to the noble associate of the Redeemer, to the Saviour of his brethren!

But the burden of the priesthood is fearful even to angels. He is laden with the weight of all the souls he has a mission to save. It is much for an angel to have to guide one soul; what will it be for one soul to have to lead thousands of others? *

In passing before the angel of a priest, I bade him joy, I treated him with honor — I could not envy him.

Whatever might be the vocation of the young man, I understood that it was his duty to follow it, and that he could not, without

* St. Thomas of Villanova, On the Angels

the greatest danger, be faithless to it. He had besought me to obtain for him a knowledge of it. I myself awaited only the revelation of the Most High.

12

XLIII.

The Vocation.

MOVED as if I were about to learn the secret of my own destiny, I flew up to heaven, and penetrated into the sanctuary. The book in which are contained the vocations of men was surrounded by angels who consulted it. Under their eyes was placed, at the moment marked, the page that interested them. They received at the same time the knowledge of the vocation and of the graces destined to make it succeed.*

I saw angels who were sad and afflicted;

* J. Marchant, Jardin des Pasteurs.

they sought new aid for souls faithless to the first graces.   One of them said to me, with sorrow :

" Salvation will still be possible to the soul intrusted to me ; but alas! it will be difficult for her!   She will no longer have the choice graces that awaited her in the way in which she was first called."

The book was at length opened for me. On the desired page I read : " A holy life in the world ; Christian marriage."

All the difficulties of this state of life grew before my eyes.   I was overwhelmed.   But the Lord, with a mildness that inspired confidence, said to me : " Open thy hands."

My hands opened, and the Lord placed in them such abundant graces that my fears vanished at once.

Among these graces some were to make the vocation known and accepted, the others to render its duties easy.

Apart from men and in solitude and in presence of his eternity, the young man learned of me the secret he had thus far sought with his prayers.

XLIV.

The Spouse.

AFTER having revealed to him his vocation to the married state, I made him know the spouse adorned with modesty, whom Heaven had destined for him.*

She had been prepared for him long before. The angel of holy unions had established those relations in the name of God, which incline one virtuous soul toward another.

The angel of the young girl and I had seconded him. We had cherished between

* J. Marchant, Jardin des Pasteurs.

these two hearts the perfect harmony, that we contemplate without seeing the consoling results.   We˙perceived the design of God only after we had been the executors of it.*

By the holiness of his conduct and the purity of his soul the young man had merited from the young girl the beautiful qualities and the virtues with which he saw her embellished.   And the young girl found a recompense for her innocence in the treasure of living faith and inexhaustible generosity the heart of the youth brought her.

What did the demon not do to hinder the accomplishment of the will of God?   He did his utmost to bring about a change, by prompting other alliances in which grace and virtue would have had no part.

At one time it was the goods of fortune he presented brilliantly, and placed in view a seductive future.   Under this deceitful veil, I showed the youth the yawning abyss: "See

* Tobias xii 3   Humbert de Romanis

that bad disposition, that heart without noble qualities, those worldly tastes."*

At another time it was the natural qualities he exalted. Exterior gifts were to triumph over all, and procure unalterable happiness. I said to the young man: "Where is piety, fear of the Lord, faithfulness to duty? Do you want a heart that will come to chill your charity by its indifference, rather than one that will sustain your virtue?"

Again, it was relationship and friendship that interfered. They made much of an alliance, that flattered their self-love and their ambition, but which would have brought destruction to the dispositions of the soul. One ray of light was enough for me to strengthen the youth, and save him from influences but little Christian.

Nothing was of any avail against the choice of Providence. If human motives had been consulted, it was in a just degree. Consider-

* St. Clement of Alexandria, Stromata. lib. 4.

ations of a higher order were supreme. Neither the egotistical calculation of material goods, nor the blind slavery of passion, nor the tyrannous pressure of the will of others, nor any means used by the devil, hindered the manifestation and the accomplishment of the Divine decrees.

XLV.

Tears.

T O the joy caused by a design formed under such favorable auspices succeeded all at once the greatest apprehension.

A marriage had been celebrated; it was that of the scandalizing friend who had failed to lead astray the young man in the days of his childhood. The youth was invited to it, and he came.

The future spouses were thought happy: they were not. A cloud of sadness darkened their soul; their hearts were in sin. They had arranged everything beforehand; all was prepared, all . . . except the one thing essen-

tial. They made a plaything of the sacrament of mercy, and they came to insult God,
before His face. The holy act that was to
have so powerful an influence on their des-
tinies for time and for eternity was about to
be changed into a crime.*

At the moment the priest pronounced the
words of the union, the blessing descended;
but not finding whereon to rest in these
tainted hearts, it went back again to heaven.

"They would not of my benediction,"
said the Most High; "it shall be withdrawn
from them; they shall have my curse." †

The curse descended in its turn; it fell
upon the guilty couple, and like an avenging
fluid passed from one to the other when they
joined hands, and penetrated to the very
marrow of their bones.‡

They were united; but in their very union
they had received the principle of the most
cruel divisions. Their bonds were one day

* Tobias vi. 16, 17.   † Ps 108.   ‡ Ibid.

to be stripped of the vain flowers that dazzled them ; they will be found made up only of sharp thorns.

The wedding crowned in a manner worthy of it the sacrilege that had just been committed. In the songs and discourses, in the attitudes and movements there was nothing but license. The demons applauded, the angels veiled their faces. Oh, how sad are the marriages from which the Lord is excluded! *

During the long hours of that day I did nothing but repeat: "Avert, O Lord! so great a calamity from him who is dear to me, and from her whom you destine for him!"

* St. Jerome, Letter to Heloidius. St. John Chrysostom, Comm. on St. Matt.

XLVI.

Confidence.

I BLESS the Lord for it still! Instead of seeing my fears realized, I felt them yielding little by little.

The arts of the Evil One failed. Not having been able to break an alliance agreeable to God, he succeeded no better in depriving it of its sublime character. Reserving for the last day his most subtle snares, he came to spread them at the entrance of the new way. But he could not gain what but too often he obtains.

The young man prepared for his marriage by prayer, and not by the follies of sin.*

* Tobias vi. 22.

Purity of intention had guided him, and he had not lowered one of the greatest acts of his life to the level of temporal interests.

The immediate preparation was such as I desired. The heart found in penance and holy works the beauty it had had on the day of first communion. With more light, it had not less innocence.

We were at the decisive hour, and we had no longer any fear. Raphael had chained Satan and kept him far from us. The festival was going to be chaste and full of pleasure. No untoward apparition was to trouble our joy.*

Tobias viii. 3.

13   K

XLVII.

The Wedding.

HEY came to the temple pure, and full of fervor. Their angels knelt at their sides. We rejoiced to see allied the traditional virtues of two excellent families, that came to bring together their treasures of good examples.

At the solemn moment the blessing came from the bosom of God. Like a river of graces, it spread itself over the hearts of the affianced pair, and made the virtues proper to their new state spring up in them.*

Love and fidelity, goodness and sweetness, happy days, and long life: it was the reunion

* Eccleasticus xxxix.

of all the good that makes up the only happiness of life, and prepares the perfect bliss of heaven.*

It put the two souls so well in harmony, that they seemed to be only one. It bound them in ties so much the sweeter, because they were so strong. Their indissolubility will be the source of charms that will never vanish.

We presented to our brothers, the angels, the act of union. In ratifying it, they showed us the part they took in our joy, and the interest they bore the spouses. Each one was eager to contribute something to their happiness, and offered some special wish for them.†

The Divine Guest was present at the modest and edifying feast that followed. He had been invited to this wedding by prayer and holiness, and brought to it that good-will we saw in him at the marriage of Cana.

---

* Humbert de Romanis   † Tertullian, Ad Uxorem, lib. 2.

The relatives and friends had addressed to Him their prayers in the temple. He loved to see them now seated together at the same table, and He strengthened the cordial relations established between the two families.*

Beginning with the next day to show Him their gratitude, the spouses made Him two visits that were unspeakably dear to Him. They visited Him in His poor on earth by their alms, and in His poor in purgatory through the Holy Sacrifice, celebrated according to their intention.

* Humbert de Romanis.

XLVIII.

The Fireside.

RARELY does earth offer to heaven a spectacle more beautiful than that of an innocent and pious family.

This one was an Eden, which we had a mission to defend against the spirit of ill, and our zeal was the flaming sword that guarded the entrance.

The spouses were mutually inclined to good. They were seen together at the church, at the tribunal of penance, at the Eucharistic table. In joy and in grief, during work or rest, they were animated by the same spirit.

In them were strength and grace, and in them virtue and piety joined hands.*

The paradise they dwelt in was going to produce magnificent flowers of innocence.†

At the sight of a new infant, I saw begin again the scenes of which I had once been a witness, and in which I had taken so delightful a part. The young soul was presented to us by her angel. He was happy to unite himself to us and enter into the family. The family numerous, numerous also are the angels.

We were in nowise strangers at the fireside. We were seen there by faith. They seemed to recognize us, and held intercourse with us. We were often blessed, consulted, thanked.‡

The familiarity of our relations was full of advantage to our friends, and had no ill consequence for us. We were able to give

* Tertullian, Ad Uxorem, lib 2
† St Clement Alex., Pedagogus, lib 2
‡ St. Lawrence Justinian, Discourse on St Michael

them our virtues without any danger of incurring their faults. How happy such friendship ! *

Their companionship soon had the character that distinguishes that of the angels. Everything in it was firmly based on affection.†

The brother, through charity, would throw over the faults of his brothers a veil of gold, through which only the good could be seen.

The father and mother made their happiness consist in their mutual devotion, and their love was like ours: what they loved, above everything, in their children, was their soul.

*St. Bernard, Comm on Ps 90
† Peter of Blois, Discourse on St Michael.

XLIX.

The Ladder.

LADDER formed of luminous rays was placed between heaven and the roof that covered this family. It was used day and night, by spirits from above, who came to visit us. The house of our friends offered them a sojourn of predilection. They looked on it as an earthly resting-place, to which they came to share our joys and increase them.*

Nothing was left undone to attract such amiable guests. Whatever could have displeased their eyes was with the greatest care kept far away.

* Life of St. Antoninus, Boll.

Disobedience, pride, discord, bad language, lawless acts, would have made them take flight.*

Purity of manners, chastity of speech, submission, humility, mutual good understanding made them forget heaven.

To repress abuse, or recall duty, one word from the father was enough:

"Do you wish, my child, to make the good angels leave the house, and deprive us of their society? Know that with the good angels come all good things, and that without them we should be exposed to all kinds of evil.†

"If heaven come down to earth, in this spot, and seems to us to be one with this blessed house, it is because innocence and virtue have attracted it to us."

---

* St. Nilus, Letter to Theodore. St. Bernard Sermon on St. Michael.

† St. Thomas of Villanova, On the Angels St. Bernard, Sermon on St. Michael. Louis of Blois, Retreat of the Faithful Soul.

L.

The Flower-Basket.

THEN, morning and evening, the members of the family, on their knees, were as one soul and one heart, to pray to God! we also were prostrate in adoration.* We joined our voices to that beautiful mingling of voices grave and of voices childlike. No one failed to be part of this pious circle. Even the angel of him who slept in his crib united with us, and prayed for his little brother.†

The demons sought to trouble the holy

---

* St. Nilus, On Prayer. Louis of Blois, Appendix to the Ascetic Life.

† St. Bernard, Meditations, ch. vi.

exercise. They came and placed themselves on the head, on the mouth, and on the eyes of our friends. 'T was then came fatigue, or sleep, or tedium, or foolish fancies, to stop the acts of the heart. We drove away the tempters, and fervor returned.*

We gathered the prayers with great care. For us they were like flowers that sprang up in the soul, and opened without through the word. We formed with them a basket of flowers.

Those from which distraction had torn no leaf, nor any profane feeling had soiled, those that were fresh and pure, intact and whole, had the place of honor.

To heighten the brilliancy of these flowers, culled in the valley of exile, we took still richer ones from the garden of our country. The flowers of heaven came to wed those of earth, and imparted to them their own fragrance and beauty.†

---

* St. Thomas of Villanova, On the Angels   Life of St. Macarius of Egypt, Boll   † St Climacus, Ladder of Heaven

Possessed of all the treasures of glory, we had nothing to ask for ourselves. But with what joy did we ask for those who were dear to us! We felt a like want of praising in our own name, and of praying in the name of our brothers. Their weakness, their sorrows, their perils, became our portion. By a touching exchange, love gave us their misery, and bestowed on them our privileges.

Embellished by our fervor, and sustained by our hands, the flower-basket was accepted as coming from our friends, and obtained for them the favors they needed.*

When thrice a day and oftener they turned to Mary and hailed her in the words of Gabriel, 't was for us to gather the pious Aves and offer them.

Mary bent to receive them with a look of tender love. She had for this embassy of earth the same smile she had for that of hea-

* St Thomas Villanova, On the Angels. Lives of SS Dorothy Arrignus, and Annowaredh, Boll

ven. She received the lowly child as she did the glorious archangel. The emotion she felt was the same she experienced the day it was announced to her that she was to become the mother of her God.

14

LI.

The Blessing.

THEY showed their trust in us by their earnestness in asking aid of us.*

Before any important enterprise, on the point of beginning any difficult work, on the eve of any dangerous journey, each one would come and prostrate himself under the hand of his angel, and would say: "I will not commence, unless you have first blessed me."†

They begged of us to bless them in the morning, that the day might be a good one

* St. Bernard, Sermon on St. Michael.
† J. Marchant, Jardin des Pasteurs.

for them; and at night, that their sleep might be without danger.

They did not address themselves to their angels only; they had recourse to those of their benefactors, of their friends, of their enemies, to those especially of sinners, whom they sought to turn aside from evil, and bring back to good.*

At the voice of the father and in his name, I would often bless the family, or the members of it that he pointed out.†

They did not have more joy in receiving, than we had in giving. How could we repel their prayer, and deceive their trust in us, when they spoke to us with so much love?‡

Our blessing was a wish of the heart. It embraced prayers we made for the success of their projects, and for the accomplishment of their desires.

We wished them spiritual prosperity:

* Practice of St. V. de Paul, of Father Balthazar Alvarez, of M. Olier.
† Genesis lviii 16. J Marchant, Jardin des Pasteurs.
‡ St. Lawrence Justinian, Discourse on St. Michael

"May vice be extirpated; may virtue flourish; may graces flow in abundance; may there dwell in your souls richness, beauty, vigor." *

We wished them material prosperity, as far as it was beneficial to their souls : " May their bodies be strong and healthy; may the fields be covered with harvests ; may wisdom guide their plans; may everything go well with them." †

In wishing our friends this prosperity, we asked it of God. God did not fail to bestow His good-will on those He saw enjoyed ours. Our prayers drew down His favors.

* Humbert de Romanis·
† St Rémi, Comm. on the Epistle to the Ephesians.

LII.

Labor.

NO sloth: each one did the task allotted him by obedience, and continual occupation protected virtue. The family were a collection of faithful workmen laboring for God, under the direction and with the concourse of angels.*

From the time God created the earth, men and angels were charged to make it bear its fruit. The pure spirits are the invisible cultivators of it in union with men.†

In giving motion to the heavenly bodies, in presiding over the play of the elements, in

* St. Augustine, Soliloquies, 26.
† Origen, Tract against Celsus.

regulating the seasons, in spreading over the
earth the rain and the dew, in dispensing
light and heat, we made the seeds germinate,
the plants grow, the flowers bloom, the fruits
ripen.*

It has happened sometimes that angels have
taken the form of men, and have come to cultivate, at his side or in his place, the fields,
to tend his flock, to build his dwelling, to
steer his vessel.†

By these exceptions in favor of some saints,
God showed that no labor was unworthy of
the noblest creatures.

Working in concert with the angels, and
seeing himself in the midst of them, the father of the family loved his condition. Every
occupation became ennobled in his eyes, and
agreeable to him. He was never seen dis-
couraged or overcome.

*Cosmas Indic. Christian Topography, lib. 2   Bail , Théologie Aff
des Anges

†Lives of SS. Isidor, Felix of Valois , of St. Raymond Nonnatus,
Cartag , Boll.

On a day of great labor the tempter said to him, ironically: " Wouldst thou be willing to sell me a drop of thy sweat?"

" Thou art too late," replied the just man; " it is not in my power to dispose of a single drop of it. I have put it out elsewhere, at so high a price, that with all the treasures of the world thou couldst not have wherewith to purchase the least drop."*

These drops of sweat had long ago been sold. I had been the promoter and the agent of the contract. I held in my hand a vase of gold which I received from God to collect them during work.†

At the end of each day I had but to breathe lightly on them, they were changed to pearls and jewels, and I hastened to attach them to the crown that awaits the faithful servant in heaven.

* Life of St. Francis of Assisium.
† St. Bernard, Sermon on St. Michael.

LIII.

Repose.

OUR care did not restrict itself to watching over the labor of the day; it was redoubled during the repose of night.*

If the father of the family never saw his sleep broken by the lurid glare of fire, if his children were always in the morning found full of health and innocence, they owed thanks for it to their guardian angels.†

When darkness covered the earth, when our friends slept, with them slept too their prudence and their strength. The senses,

---

* St Bernard, Meditations, 6.
† James Alvarez, Tr. on the Religious Life, b. 1.

weighed down by the duties of the day, ceased to watch. The citadel was open; Satan was ready to rush to it.

That friend of night, who multiplies himself in its shades that he may inspire unholy designs, sharpen the dagger of the assassin, light the torch of the incendiary, came to place himself above the couch where virtue reposed. Even in sleep he tormented it, and made it feel his deadly influence.*

Our light alone restricted the power of the accursed one. We repelled the dangerous phantoms evoked in the midst of dreams, and overcame their effects by heavenly images.

How many evils did we ward off from those roofs that had become our own!

Notwithstanding his love and our vigilance, God could have permitted some accident; but without our watchfulness and His love, our brothers would not for an instant

* St. Augustine, Serm. 4

have been able to save themselves from the devil.*

Under our wings the repose of night was taken without fear. It renewed and sanctified them just as did the labor of the day. The offering they had made of it to God gave the soul an impulse, that bore it onward in the way of merit, even when the body was inactive and gave itself up to the sleep it needed.†

* St. Bernard, Comm. on 90th Ps.
† James Alvarez, Tr. on Relig. Life, 2.

LIV.

Raise Your Heart to God.

OVER the dwelling of innocence was heard the sound of rejoicing, and in the air angelic voices spoke: "Behold, behold, it is the day of the Lord!" 'T was Sunday.

The arms ceased their movement, all work was suspended. From midnight to midnight they were to have rest.

The angels that lead the stars have no need of ceasing from outward action that they may praise God. More distracted, our friends could not join their material occupations with the praises of God. It was not asking too much of all their attention that it should be directed to the spectacle that was offered to their faith, and be called on to discharge the duties that were prescribed for them.

On the Lord's day the air clothed itself, in their sight, with a more heavenly tint, and nature spoke to them a language more touching. In this verdure and in these flowers, in this light and in these clouds everything had life. Each object breathed a pure incense, and from all sides came mysterious invitations: " Raise your hearts to God!"

Our inspirations disclosed to them, even in the least creature, a way of raising their thoughts to the Author of all.

On each flowret of the valley there rested a souvenir of piety. 'T was the Passion-flower, the Dream of Heaven, the Crown of the Angels, the Virgin's Eyes, the Smile of the Infant Mary, the Ave, the Blood of Jesus.*

* Popular names of flowers.

The voice of the little bird had its language in which to speak to them of God. The sparrow, in mounting heavenward, and in singing, under the azure vault, its hymn of thanks, called thither their look and their thoughts.

On the hill-side, in the shade of a grove, on the border of a stream, on the top of a mountain, they breathed a perfumed air that came from the hills of heaven.

The material world was for them a Divine manuscript, of which they knew the origin and the authenticity. We taught them to seize the spiritual sense of it, hidden under each phenomenon. We helped them read in the firmament and in the stars, as on earth and in the flowers, the brilliant characters traced by the hand of the Almighty.

But had their eyes been opened to the light of glory, they would have seen the country more richly enamelled, and the air traversed by more harmonious legions. The

15

angels would have appeared to them not only going from one pole to another, but from star to star, from sun to sun, and filling space with their splendors and with their canticles.*

* St. Ambrose, Comm on St. Luke   Life of St Colombanus, Boll.

LV.

The Holy Sacrifice.

ON the Lord's day the law of repose set aside profane works, and the law of worship called for holy ones. They came to group themselves around the work by excellence, the Holy Sacrifice.

At the moment the Saviour was going to offer himself as a holocaust, our friends, in obedience to a precept dear to the heart, hastened to wend their way to the church, the meeting-place of heaven and earth.

On entering, we bent before the priest, who was preparing to mount the altar, and then before the guardian spirits of the holy place.

When the representative of Jesus Christ advanced to the new Calvary, angels went before him, others followed him, all assisted him in his holy office.*

We repeated in the invisible world the prayers and the canticles of men. We alternated with them in supplication and in praise. Like them and for them we repeated with sighs, "Lord have mercy on us!" And soon, our voice resuming its vigor, we sang as at Bethlehem: "Glory to God in the highest, and peace on earth to men of good-will!"

At the name of Jesus all the hierarchy bent the knee. The evil spirits wandering over the earth or chained in the abyss, did in like manner, but by force, and in spite of themselves.†

When about to accomplish the great act of consecration, the priest called on those present to give thanks with the angels, and

* Lives of St Catherine of Bologna, St Felix of Valois, St Ignatius of Antioch, Boll
† Life of St Frances of Rome, Boll

unite themselves to the Redeemer. He bowed profoundly and said: "Holy! Holy! Holy!" and all heaven prostrate repeated with him: "Holy! Holy! Holy is the Lord, the God of armies!"*

The altar was then covered with lights and burning incense, that transformed it into a glowing pyre of love.†

From each choir of heaven came new spirits to offer, like ourselves, to His Father the tender Lamb that takes away the sins of the world. At the sight of this only object of his complacency, the Most High showed but clemency and bounty.‡

We addressed ourselves to the Saviour and said to him: "Thanks for those whom you have prevented by your love, even to giving yourself for them on the cross."§

* Philip the Solitary, Letter to the Monk Callinus. Life of St. Catherine of Bologna, Boll.

† Life of St Clement of Ancyra, Boll.

‡ St. J Chrysostom, Tr. on the Priesthood, b 6. St Gregory the Great, Dialogues, b 4. St Ambrose, Comm. on St Luke. Life of St. Veronica, Boll.

§ St J. Chrysostom, On the Incomprehensibility of God.

15 *

All the treasures of mercy were opened and given to us. Sunday had drawn from the adorable Sacrifice the holiness that was to be transmitted to the days of the week, as the heart sends blood and life to the members of the body.

LVI.

The Profaners of the Holy Day.

THE fidelity of our friends was not without its trial. They had for a long time under their eyes a family of profaners, who forgot the church on the holy day and gave themselves up to guilty labor.

"Do they not prosper as well as you?" said Satan. "Are their fields less fertile than yours, their meadows less verdant, their flocks less healthy, their springs less plentiful, their vines less generous? Is their look not smiling, and does not everything turn out for them as they wish? Disabuse yourselves: take possession again of a day that you sacrificed to a chimera."

Our friends had not a clear sight to see, as we do, the secrets of sovereign justice, and understand the mystery of its slowness; but the liveliness of their faith, and the light we gave them, were enough to lay bare these lies.

To their eyes the house of profanity sent up a dark vapor to heaven that called down vengeance; the house of piety gave forth a grateful incense that mounted up to gain a blessing.*

Benediction and vengeance did not come down to rest only on the upturned soil and make it fertile or barren.   They fell upon souls, and produced effects the most excellent or the most disastrous.

'T is left to eternity to punish the sins of time or to reward its virtues.

The father of the family saw, in spirit, countless scourges dart down upon a land.

* Rupert, Comm on the Apocalypse, b. 5

He beheld storms blast the harvest, winds corrupt the fruits, diseases strike down the strongest health, tombs open on all sides.

" Behold," said I, " what the avenging breath leaves after it, as it passes over the spot where profanity reigns! 'T is God, who retakes from the goods and life of man, what has been unjustly refused Him or violently taken from Him. There, however, mercy is still to be seen. These scourges are as much warnings as punishments. But turn and see."

The father of the family turned, and saw Divine Justice erect, drawing a bow, and pointing the shaft at the breast of a man who stood face to face with it. Far from flying, the madman pretended indifference, and seemed to suspect no danger. Temporal prosperity and impunity had put a bandage on his eyes. The longer the arrow is in leaving the bow the more terribly will it fly. The wound will be incurable, the pain eternal.   Such is the lot of the impious man, allowed in time to go unpunished.*

Penetrated with compassion at this sight, the father of the family repeated the wise saying he had received from his fathers, and which he was to bequeath to his children :

"'T is folly to refuse God what He asks, or to take what he refuses."

* St. Jerome, St. Chrysostom, Life of St. Geneviève, Boll.

LVII.

God's Part.

THE part of God and of his poor was on every side, amid the possessions of our friends. It hung from the tree, it waved in the field of wheat, it coursed in the vine, it budded in the soil. We saw it in the milk of the flock, in the honey of the bee, in the fleece of the sheep, in the stalk of the flax.

While the poor man sated his hunger, under this roof so hospitable, warmed his members, clothed himself in a new garment, or, took his rest, his angel overflowed with

thanksgiving, and sang his hymn of gratitude.*

How many guardian angels passed by in
this way, and were able to admire the Christian faith and the goodness of heart that distinguished this family!

It happened one day that a stranger seemed
to take upon himself the work of wearying
out such touching generosity. Scarcely had
he left, when he returned with new laments.
Far from lessening, the aid each time became
more abundant.   All at once the face of the
stranger shone, his garments became radiant,
two beautiful wings opened, the angel took
his flight, and went to tell in heaven what
he had seen on earth.†

But not only men and angels came to
knock at the door of this dwelling: Jesus
Christ Himself crossed its threshold.   He it
was who, in the person of the poor, had re-

* Life of St. Ambrose of Siena, Boll

† Lives of St. Gregory the Great, St. Zita, St. Ailus, St. Edward,
Boll.

ceived alms, been lodged, fed, clothed, comforted, and consoled.*

Our friends had no false ideas on this point. Their house having been for some days without this Divine Visitor, they became sorrowful. "They come to us no longer," they would say; "perhaps we have offended them." The arrival of a poor man gave them new joy.†

The sight of such charity enraged Satan. He sought at first to taint it by means of the poison of self-love. How many insinuations, how many subtle deceptions, to this end! But the friends of God remained as humble as they were devoted.

He hoped to dishearten them by making impostors present themselves. He himself did not hesitate to play this hypocritical part. The father of the family having given alms to an unknown person, the man threw off his

* St. Matthew xxv.
† Life of the Ven- Louis of Blois

rags, and showed himself clad in silk and gold, crying out in a formidable voice: "Know that thou hast given an alms to Satan." "I have given it for the love of my God," replied the father of the family, "and it is into His hand that my mite has fallen."

LVIII.

The Value of Alms.

THE poor man succored, a touching spectacle was presented to us. The Saviour appeared in the midst of the angels, and showed them the piece of bread, the glass of water, the coin, the scrap of cloth, saying:

" My servants have done me this act of charity." *

Seen in the glare of the world, these objects were vulgar and common; beheld in the brightness of heaven, they were rich and brilliant. Charity gave them their price. The

* Life of St. Martin of Tours. Sulpitius Severus.

wool of sheep changed into a regal robe, the
glass of water became a cup of enchantment,
the humble penny a piece of gold, the morsel
of bread excelled in whiteness and sweetness
the manna of angels.

But the marks of respect and affection, the
alms of the heart, found the Divine alms-
seeker moved yet more. What transports
when, showing us the scar of His foot or of
His hand, Jesus said to us:

"There have their lips been pressed." *

We were filled with a sense of our glory,
and with courage at hearing cherished names
pronounced before the choirs of angels, and
to see the looks of all directed to us.

"'T is a beautiful thing," we said, "to bless
God in His glory, and to sing His praises
in our home; but how much more beautiful
to assist Him in His distress, and console
His sorrow in exile!"

The part reserved for God, in these fields,

* Life of St. Jerome Emilian, of St John of God, Boll.

brought down on them His blessing, and turned away scourges. With the movement of a wing the angels drove off the storms, and under their breath the air became pure and healthy. To save the portion of Jesus Christ, they saved that of the family.

But these favors, procured by almsgiving, and which God sometimes withholds through motives of a higher order, were hardly a part payment. The debt was to be paid only at the last day, when the Sovereign Judge will call together the nations, to give to each one according to his works.

Our dearest wish was to see these debts multiply. As faithful agents, we entered in the great book acts of mercy and of charity, even to the least of them.

16 *

LIX.

The Trial.

THE plant we were cultivating presented a wonderful phenomenon. While to the eyes of the angels and of heaven it was crowned with flowers, in its earthly aspect and to the eyes of men it bristled with thorns. If the thorns were long, sharp, tearing, the flowers were striking, brilliant, and fragrant. The thorns and flowers were nourished by the same sap, and had the same spring. The name of this plant was Christian Virtue.*

When our friends felt the point of the thorns, they were tempted to break them.

* A thought expressed by Pius IX. at Gaeta.

186

We prevented them; they would have killed the flowers.

"It is good," we told them, "that exile should not be too enchanting; one would cease from sighing and repeating the name of his absent country."

Like to the shrubs of the East that give out their hidden perfumes only when they are bruised, their hearts were not to exhale the good odor of their virtue save in the bosom of trial.

Wishing to see this virtue grow and become purified, we asked for them of the Lord two sorts of blessings that in the desires of the saints are never separated: Trouble and suffering, patience and love.

The tribulation God was going to send them was a mark of predilection. With as much truth as Raphael said to Tobias, we could say to them: "Because you were acceptable to God, it was needful that temptation should try you." *

* Tobias xii. 13

I laid a cross on the shoulders of the father of the family. He kissed it, thanked God who sent it him, and trusted in my aid not to fall under its weight. From that moment I became his Cyrenean.

The pressure of suffering forced from his heart only the oil of perfect resignation, with no mixture of the murky scum of blasphemy.*

Never had he been so noble and so beautiful. Trial had given him a resemblance to the Redeemer that we did not find even in the most sublime spirits.†

It was sweet to realize in others what we could not do in our own case.

"To suffer!" we said, "to suffer for God! oh! how happy are those who enjoy such a privilege. We shall receive then always, O Lord, and never make any return! We shall be overwhelmed with the excess of Thy goodness, and not be able to show our gratitude by sacrifice and by sorrow! If we

* St Chrysostom, St Augustine
† Bossuet. On the Guardian Angels

stretch forth our hands to offer tears, they fall not from our eyes; if we lay sighs at Thy feet, they come not up from our hearts; if we present the sweat of the brow, it is not of ours; if we place on the altar of sacrifice one drop of blood, it did not start from our veins. In the holocaust of suffering we have seen man and God. The angel alone has never been a victim!" *

* St Bernard, Sermon on St. Michael

LX.

The Angels of the Family.

WHEN different seeds are intrusted to the bosom of the
earth, they receive but the
same sun and the same dew.
Each flower, however, that springs
out from it, has its own perfume and
its own colors.

So was it with these numerous children.
Fed at the same breast, fondled on the knees
of the same mother, formed by an education
common to all, they soon showed different
tendencies. The spirit of God breathing in
different directions inspired a variety of

vocations. The guardian angels by this saw their various tasks marked out.

The distance that the Divine will placed between the brothers, as they advanced in age, did not separate us. We remained united, and were the bond that kept them from isolating themselves.

They could correspond through us, under the eye of God, and transmit to each other the pledges of their affection. The mutual communication they kept up of their spiritual goods did not suffer from distance; it was prompt, instantaneous.

There existed a sweet relation between the angels of the family. What interested one interested all. They consulted together often on the means of providing for the common good, and for private wants.

As angel of the father, I was no stranger either to the children or to their angels. The emotions of my brothers were mine: their joys were my joys, their sadness my own. Never did my heart cease to beat in unison with theirs.

LXI.

The Poems.

EACH one of us wrote a poem on the supernatural life of a soul. There was the poem of the father, of the mother, those of the children, of the servant.* Our friends furnished us, by their virtues, the subject of our recitals and of our songs. From our pen flowed the heavenly poetry that embellished all. A thought, a word, a sigh, a tear, the least movement was precious to us. We hastened to cut the brilliant, polish it, and place it where it could shine with greatest lustre.†

* St. Thomas of Villanova, On the Angels.
† St. Jerome, Comm. on Ecclesiastes. St. Basil of Cæsarea, Hom. on Fasting. St. Bernard, Meditations, 6.

Divine grace was the principle of all good. It alone gave fertility to souls and made their beauties bud forth. With what solicitude did we not induce hearts to follow its inspirations.*

In the poem we told of the unaffected piety of childhood, the ardent generosity of youth, the incorruptible fidelity of ripe age, the sweet resignation of advanced years.†

Its perfection did not depend either on the outward distinction of life, or on the length of it. It came from the merit of the subject before God. A few full days gave matter for a masterpiece; long, fruitless years would have left us in indigence.

At times of laxity, what deplorable pages! In the better days of penance, we corrected, effaced, placed in light the good freed from evil.

The angel poets have not all to fulfil a

* Richard of St. Victor, Comm. on Cant. of Canticles.
† Life of St. John of God, Boll.

task equally consoling. One human life is a flow of beautiful actions, another a tissue of crimes. The first presents only generous aspiration and magnanimous efforts; the second offers but barren desires and cowardly longings.

The poem of which a proud revolt will have been the last word shall be condemned of inexorable justice, and given over to the devils to be the objects of their everlasting raillery.

The one that will have been crowned by an humble submission shall be exalted by mercy. The angel who wrote it shall recite it solemnly in the assembly of the elect, in honor of him who will have been the hero of it.

This history of his whole life, dictated by the just man to his guardian angel, will be the only fortune that shall accompany him out of the visible world.*

When in the midst of the last shipwreck

* Apocalypse xiv 13

he will swim toward the heavenly shore,
above his head and on the wing of his angel
he shall see his poem, that is, his treasure,
his glory, his immortality.

LXII.

The Angel of the Little Chosen One.

I.

ISFORTUNE has come," they told us; "a terrible blow has struck the friends of God."

Death had come to carry off the youngest of the children, and upon the knee of the mother was seen only a lifeless body.

Through these scenes of mourning the angel guardian had contemplated a most sweet spectacle; he had seen the hand of God take up from the earth a young plant, and bear it off to heaven.

The storm would have broken it to pieces.

17 *

Men did not foresee this; but He, to whom everything is present, made it known to the angel who cultivated it. To save it, God had hastened to put it out of danger. On the banks of the living waters of paradise, it will flourish in a perpetual spring.

The mother shed tears, but the Church, clad in white vestments of joy, sang: "Praise the Lord, ye children." *

And the children of heaven took up the refrain that had been said for each of them: "He was taken away, lest malice should corrupt his spirit or vanity lead astray his soul." †

They added, in pointing out his budding virtues and his rapid progress in good: "In a few days he finished a long course." ‡

The angels came in great numbers to receive him, and lead him to the crowd of innocents that were playing with their crowns and their palms before the altar of the Lamb.§

* Ps cxii 1.   † Wisdom iv. 11   ‡ Ibid iv 13.
§ St Theresa, To a mother who had lost her little child   St Francis de Sales, To a mother who had likewise lost hers   Hymn of the poet Prudentius

The Saviour said, at the sight of him: "Suffer this little child to come to me." And he bestowed with prodigality caresses, embraces, and blessings.*

II.

Hardly had the child entered heaven, clinging always to the hand of his angel, and almost as beautiful as he, when he turned to look on his father, his mother, and his brothers.

In tears they were burying his body. Had God allowed him, he would have had but to show himself in the brilliant light with which he was shining; every tear would have been dried up.

He often came to take his place at the fireside, whither he brought treasures of grace: he was the new saint of the family, and one of its protectors. He was its glory and ornament.†

* St. Mark x 14, 16
† Life of St. Gregory Nazianzen, Boll.

Far from having lost anything, his affection had become more lively. A tear in the eyes of his mother, a drop of sweat on the brow of his father, the slightest cloud of sadness on the face of one of his brothers, touched him, and caused the sweetest outpourings of his love.

He heard them, he was there when they spoke of him, when they recalled his smile, his candor, his engaging ways, and when they said:

"He would be so old to-day; he would resemble such a child; he would praise such an action, rejoice at such an event, share in such a favor. What grief to see him no more! But he is in the bosom of God, and can have the company of his relations, who will have without doubt recognized him, although they never saw him on earth."

Guided by the guardian angel, a hand traced on the tomb: *

*Life of St Agatha, Boll.

"Of such is the kingdom of Heaven!"

Nowhere more willingly did the birds come to sport, to sing their carols, and hang the nest of their little ones in the green leaves that shaded the spoils of innocence.

In the midst of the shrubbery that interlaced its branches, the youngest brother had planted some violets and cultivated them. A beautiful lily grew there, and ever after was renewed each spring.*

* Life of St. Aureus and Companions, of St. William Infant, of St. Agatha, of St. Hildegarde, Boll.

LXIII.

The Angel of the Virgin.

I.

HE rustle of a leaf, a voice in the night, a fancied apparition when alone, made the young girl grow pale. Her angel did not try to undeceive her: "It is," said he, "a saving timidity and fear." *

One day, when the demon of vanity sought to tarnish her soul, he found her deaf to flattery and falsehood.

Innocence shone on her brow; modesty covered her breast; wisdom guarded her

* St. Ambrose, Comm. on St. Luke. St. Bernard, Comm. on Text " Missus est."

heart; no frivolous expressions escaped her lips.*

An exquisite sensibility marked her piety, and candor gave her virtue a most touching character.

The foul spirit thought to gain possession of a heart at once tender and affectionate. He chose a sharp arrow, dipped it in poison, and shot it. Under a frail and delicate body was a soul of adamant, and the arrow, blunted, fell harmless. By plunging this soul into the fires of charity, the angel had made her invulnerable.

The young girl disdained bodily beauty, which too often gives joy to the Evil One; but she was jealous of beauty of soul, which comes from the carefully preserved image of God. She fled from anything that could mar that image, brushed the dust from it, and left nothing undone to increase its bril-

*Tertullian, De Veland. Virg. et de Ornatu Muliebri, Boll.

liancy. She shone with all the beauty proper
to holy souls.*

Her angel was seen in her features, in her
eyes, in her bearing. He brought with him
and inspired reserve, purified her looks or
made them turn elsewhere. He was in relation with the angels of Cecily, of Agnes, of
Thecla, of all the heroines of Divine love.†

Jesus said to the angel: "This heart
pleases _me; I wish to hold it undivided.
To thee is given to prepare it for its early
union with me."

II.

Few souls understand the Divine secret;
so few seek after it and make themselves
worthy of it! ‡

"It is," said the angel to the young girl,
"a pearl that the world despises, and which

* Life of St Gregory Nazianzen, Boll.

† St. Ambrose, De Virginibus, l. 3. Lives of SS. Ida Infant, and
Ozanna, Boll

‡ St. Matt xix. 11.

I value more than the universe; that corrupt souls tread under foot, and pure hearts buy at the price of every sacrifice; that the impious treat as a vain, chimerical, useless object, and the saints call the honor of the body, the glory of the soul, the riches of the Church, the ornament of angels, the garment of the favorites of God.*

" This pearl is not hidden in the depths of the sea, it is not lying in the bowels of the earth; it is in the midst of men; it brings them innumerable goods they pass unnoticed.

"Guess what is this peerless pearl, and tell me what is its beautiful name."

The young girl had named virginity. She had recognized it by features it shares with no other virtue.

The sight of it had given her an ardent desire to have it.

The angel wished to make the desire more lively; he added:

* St. Athanasius, De Virginitate. St. Jerome, Tr. cont. Jov., b. 2.

18

"Dost thou see that meadow, part of which is set out for pasturage of flocks, a part is ravaged by unclean animals, and the third part is untouched?

"The first offers still to the view its carpet of green, but it has no longer the graceful beauty the variety of flowers gave it: it represents the heart bound by the ties of marriage.

"The aspect of the second is desolate and repelling. It has no verdure, no freshness: it represents a heart enslaved by impure passions.

"Nothing has ruined the beauty of the third. The herbage is tall and tender, the flowers are bright and sweet-smelling, the fruits savory and plentiful: 'tis the symbol of the heart vowed to virginity.

"Contemplate virginity in this light, and judge if it be worthy of possessing thy heart." *

* Life of St. Martin of Tours. Sulpitius Severus.

The young girl vowed to have no other spouse but Christ.

III.

The angel was the paranymph of this alliance. It was made in the midst of the world, but far from profane eyes. Everything took place in the secret of the heart. Pure spirits only celebrated this unseen wedding. They presented to the bride a veil ornamented with lilies, and the Saviour put on her finger a ring of gold.*

In the judgment of worldlings her life was to be a perpetual widowhood; in the judgment of the angels it passed into a most prosperous union.

The virgin had ever in view only the good pleasure of her Spouse, and the interests of His glory.†

Did the angel direct her glance to the pages wherein are told the conquests of the

* Lives of SS Angela, Agnes, Juetta, Ida, Aldegunda, Boll
† St Augustine, Tr de Virginitate.

cross? She sighed after the happiness of sacrifice. Did she hear of an outrage offered to virtue, she would have been willing to expiate it with her blood.

Jesus well deserved such fidelity. Had He not first chosen her for his spouse, and made her share his inheritance?

She had not forgotten the day on which He had appeared to her holding in one hand a crown of flowers, and in the other, one of thorns, and saying to her: "For which is thy preference?"

"As Thou, O Jesus!" she answered, "I too will circle on earth my brow with the diadem of suffering. In heaven alone, through your infinite mercy, shall I have the crown of glory."

The efforts of the world and those of Satan were not able to shake her constancy. In the presence of seductive objects the angel said to her:

"What spouse is so rich and so beautiful,

so faithful and so good as He of thy choice? What other will give answer never to quit, even in death, her who has given Him her heart?

"Jesus is the ocean of all true love, He is the source of it; wilt thou leave the ocean and source for a turbid drop that is already evaporating?"

IV.

The words of the angel never ceased coming to the mind of the virgin, and gave birth to bright thoughts and generous sentiments:

. "Thou shalt not remain isolated. Virginity is fruitful. No mother ever had so many children as the spouse of Christ. The children of the Divine Master shall be thine. Thou shalt have for a family the unfortunate."*

To the virgin this language was grateful.

* St. Augustine, Confessions, b. 8, ch. xi.

If there was a sick person to visit, a poor man to succor, an afflicted soul to cheer up, an ignorant mind to instruct, a sinner to save from the abyss: " Here," she would say, " is a portion that comes to me. I recognize in these souls the livery of my Spouse." *

A more than motherly tenderness inclined her toward those deserted, and made her look on heroic devotedness as simple and ordinary. Free from all earthly hindrance, she allowed herself to be led by a higher love, hastened to every human ill, and gave herself up without relaxation to the practices of charity. Sweet lamb of heaven, she thought not of herself, but for others covered herself with a rich fleece of good works.†

Her motherhood, coming from her union with Jesus, had nothing of nature in it. It belonged to a higher order, and came from

---

* Life of St Bonna, Boll.   † Life of St Adelard, Boll.

grace. It was pure, constant, invincible. Its character was Divine, and deeds of good could not exhaust its outpourings.

Like so many others who had gone before her in the same paths, the virgin was to exclaim, one day:

"Whence come to me all these children? Behold the family virginity gives me! O my heavenly Spouse! with what generosity have you acted toward me, and what a crown have you formed for me! I understand now that if temporal unions people the earth, the spiritual union does more; it adopts those the world repulses, gives them titles of nobility, and fills heaven with them.*

V.

The courage shown by the virgin, during her life, merited, at her death, a special recompense.

To deny everything to passion, to give all

* St. Cyprian, Tr. on Discipline and Conduct of Virgins.

to God; to bind in chains the strong tendencies of a rebellious body, to secure the triumph of the law; to remain incorruptible
and pure in the midst of a dust that soils
and taints; to anticipate the wonders of the
last day, and from the present moment put
one's self in the condition of spirits: such is
the endeavor of virginity.*

What human courage could accomplish
it? What profane virtue would dare attempt it!

There are three kinds of courage that God
rewards in eternity by a distinctive mark:
the courage of the doctor, the courage of the
martyr, and the courage of the virgin.

This sign is an accidental brightness of
the body and soul, which is called the
aureola.†

Luminous color, or colored light, the
aureola is white in the virgins, red in the

* St. Augustine, Tr. on Virginity, ch. xiii. St. Basil.
† St. Thomas, Supplement, q 96, art. 11.

martyrs, and tending to green in the doctors.*

The aureola of the doctor is made up of radiant stars, that of the martyrs of brilliant gems, that of the virgins of enchanting flowers.

The virgins hold lilies in their hands, the martyrs palms, the doctors laurels.†

Crowned with her aureola, and bearing her lily, the virgin was called to take her place on the triumphal car of her Spouse. She came thither to mingle in our ranks, and began her course through the heavens, following everywhere the Divine Lamb, and singing like us the canticle reserved for virgins and angels.‡

* Henriquez Tr. on the End of Man, ch xxvii. ₴ 8.
† Dom. Soto, Summa Quarta, Dissert. 49
‡ Apocalypse xiv. 3, 4

LXIV.

The Angel of the Soldier.

I.

T HE soldier loved his country. This land on which the temporal destiny of his ancestors was fulfilled, where the trophies of their honor were set up, where their memory is cherished, where their remains repose, where their language is spoken, where their laws rule, where their faith lives — this land was dear to the soldier's heart, and he could not hear tell of its glories without emotion.

He has made beforehand the sacrifice of his life to it. He will defend it at the price of his blood. She is a mother who has borne him in her bosom, who has educated him, who has given him a name.of which he is proud. She can count on him, and dispose of his arm; but the country of this earth will not make him forget the country of heaven: to this belongs the preference that superiority claims.

The one has rulers that perish, the other an immortal Monarch; the one has decrees of a day, the other laws immutable; the one has a banner made glorious by the sword, the other a standard made illustrious by virtue; the one has a profane past, the other sacred traditions; the one keeps the inanimate ashes of his ancestors, the other has their living souls; the one gives crowns that fade, the other laurels that are ever green; the one has time, the other eternity.

The angel taught the soldier his duties toward his two countries, and showed him that to betray one was never a means of serving the other. He made him understand

the alliance between holiness and courage,
liberty and obedience, purity and honor

The soldier was animated with the noblest
sentiments.　His soul had nothing gross or
brutal.　The innocence of his heart was read
in the severity of his brow.　One would have
said he was a spirit like those God once sent
under the exterior of shining horsemen, to
encourage and free His people.*

II.

He was soon obliged to march against the
enemy.　The news of the approaching combat did not make him fear.

From the moment the signal was given,
the angels of the Christian heroes came to
hover over the field of battle and applaud
the deeds of valor.†

When the body of a hero fell, his soul
flew toward the countless witnesses of his
devotedness.　All welcomed her with honor,

---

* Lib II. Machab xi. 8.
† II. Machab v 2　St Thomas Villanova, On the Angels

and congratulated her in having braved death. He who had inspired her and sustained her, bore her company everywhere. 'T was he who led her to the Just Judge of intentions and of acts, to the magnificent remunerator of every virtue.*

But when the impious soldier received the mortal blow, what a spectacle! " Woe! woe to him!" cried the angel in fleeing the scene of mourning. The demons only had the right to claim the soul of one who, with the most foolish inconsistency, had refused to give himself to his heavenly country, in devoting himself for that of earth.

While his glory was proclaimed, and immortality was decreed him among men, his soul was loaded with a weight of ignominy, and she saw herself condemned to a death everlasting at the tribunal of God.

Oh! how she would have preferred that her body, her name, her devotedness had re-

* St. Thomas Villanova, On the Angels.

19

mained lost and unknown among men, and
that a throne had been prepared for her
among the pure souls in heaven! For not
having directed her look and ambition high
enough, she had made the greatest of sacrifices, without profit to herself.

The angel did not see his young hero
crowned, in this first combat. Death spared
him; but it was only to reserve him for
other perils, and, through them, for greater
triumphs.

The assaults he was about to undergo in
time of peace were not to be less terrible for
his virtue.

In repelling them he merited a nobler
laurel than if he had broken the lines of the
enemy. The most beautiful of his victories
was not that which he shared with his companions in arms, but what he knew how to
win, alone, over himself and over his passions.

The angel of the country loved in a special manner this soldier and his angel. Thanks to them, and those like them, he was able to lead to its sublime destiny the great and illustrious nation over which he had been placed.

LXV.

The Angel of the Religious.

HIS guardian angel one day said to this child so peaceful and collected:

"Come into the desert, and under the protection of the walls of the cloister; 't is there God wishes thee, and to it His voice calls thee."

"Shut myself up for life!" cried the child.

"There is nothing astonishing," replied the angel, "if the doves of the cell refuse to light any more upon a soiled world: but fear not; this nest of love is only so well closed below, that it may be the better open above toward heaven." *

" To cut myself off from every one!"

"Thou breakest off thy relations with men only to have more intimate ones with the blessed spirits. The distance between the cell and heaven is not great." †

" Obedience seems to me so hard!"

" By obedience thou wilt acquire wings like ours, and thou wilt become quick and active in doing the will of God."

" Who would not be frightened at such stripping one's self of everything?"

"Thou wilt renounce the possession of even an atom of dust; but thou shalt have, like us, in change, Him who possesses worlds."

" Chastity is the privilege of a very few!"

" God destines those for it whom He cherishes with a more tender love. By it

---

* St. Thomas of Villanova, De Expectatione Partus.
† Blessed Guigues, Carthusian, Letter to Brothers of Mont Dieu.

19 *

thou wilt withdraw thyself from all attraction of the flesh, and thou wilt place thyself in the midst of us, to be attracted but by our common centre, infinite holiness." *

" Will prayer be my occupation day and night?"

" Thou shalt have ever in thy hands the harp of David, to chase away the evil spirits and call Jesus with His joys and delights.

" In heaven we praise God continually, and this praise is so sweet to us that without it we could not be happy." †

" How coarse this habit is!"

" It will only strike the eyes of those thou shouldst not seek to please. To the eyes of the angels thou wilt wear the brilliant garments of those heavenly lilies that labor not nor spin, but which eclipse by their splendor the magnificence of all the Solomons."

" There is nothing in this rule but severity and hardship."

---

* Tertullian, Ad Uxorem, lib 1. St Chrysologus, Serm. 143. Petrus Cantor, Verbum Abbreviatum.

† St. Chrysostom, Comm on Ps 41.

"It is a model of great virtue and of high perfection. How many souls has it made worthy of heaven!"

"Will it be then the life of an angel I must lead?"

"Thou shalt live our life; thou wilt gain our strength and our beauty; thou wilt be one of those legions of earthly angels so often visited by their brothers of heaven. Thy life will be as a clear stream, flowing over a bed of azure and of stars, and clothing its banks with sweet-smelling flowers."*

II.

The cloister opened to the novice. The first days brought him only consolation. Prayer, silence, labor, separation from the world — everything pleased him. But Satan was to have his turn.

A moment came when everything seemed

---

* Baldwin of Canterbury, On the Cenobitic Life. James Alvarez On the Religious Life, b. 1, ch. xii St Jerome, Letter to Eustochium.

veiled in crape. All was dark, sad, hope-less, and the youth was already saying :

"Why bind myself to a kind of life for which I feel no attraction ? Cannot one save himself in the world as well as here ? Still, even if I had a little encouragement! but it seems to me that God himself rejects me, and bids me quit this house."

"Take courage," said his guardian angel, with gentleness; "recognize the last efforts of Satan. He must fear very much thy presence in this cloister, that he should strive so to get thee out of it. Be firm. God has spoken to thee by the mouth of those who. represent him: that should be enough for thee." *

The young man kept his cell, and his cell became to him a delightful paradise.†

At the moment he pronounced his vows before God, some champions of the world pitied him ; but the angels applauded him,

* Life of St. Opportuna, Boll   † Imit. of J. C., b. 1, ch xx.

and surrounded this ceremony with great pomp.

From their joy, it would have been said that the young religious had entered into one of their choirs to be the ornament of it, and that the sacred hierarchy counted one angel more.*

III.

The religious was tormented still at times by temptation; but he was bred to war, and gained as many victories as he had to stand attacks. It happened that he felt sometimes jealousy of the preference shown for one of his brethren. The angel forthwith placed under the eyes of his spirit on one side a heap of gold, and on the other some few pieces: " Compare what each of you has left in the world; see how much the sacrifice of thy brother exceeds thine, and how inferior thou art to him in merit." †

* Lives of Blessed Baptista of Varano, of St. Juette, Boll.
† Life of St. Columbanus, Boll

P

Ambition troubled his repose. He caught himself considering in his imagination the goods that he would have been able to get together by persevering labor in the midst of men. The angel made him see in a ray of light an obscure atom that vanished in an instant. "There," said he to him, "behold the value of the universe to a soul that is immortal." *

He complained of his dryness. The angel said to him:

" When the Divine Master fled across the desert, happy were those who ceased not to follow Him. They proved to Him that their aspirations were pure, and that they had only Him in view. For these latter were reserved his predilection and caresses."

Prevented by illness, he regretted not being able to go to the choir to sing the Divine office. The regret pleased the angel, who said to him: " I will go to offer in thy place the incense of prayer."

* Life of St Benedict. Boll

To inspire him with a greater horror of temptation, the angel wished to show him the tempter himself. He made Satan appear to him in a slight flash that furrowed a cloud. "Death! death rather than such a sight!" cried the religious. "And yet," said the angel to him, "thou hast not truly seen him. The quickness of his passage has not let thee judge of his hideousness." "It matters not," said the religious; "rather than see him again thus, I should be willing to walk barefoot, to the day of judgment, on a mass of live coals." *

IV.

His holy life was of great assistance to souls remaining in the world. Thousands of voices found an echo in the cell, and from every side came angels flying, to bring the cries of distress.

The guardian angel gave them the favors

* Lives of St Catharine of Bologna, of St. Bridget, Boll.

obtained by the humble servant of God.   In times of languor and of negligence the angel, somewhat saddened, had to put in the hands of the heavenly seekers only a feeble succor· but in days of faithfulness and devotion he felt exceeding joy — he could give largely.

He soon saw the fruit of these merits.

One night a storm was raging on the ocean. A whole fleet saw death before them. "Courage," cried the chief; "it is midnight: 't is the hour when the religious rises to go to choir. Before my departure, I recommended the expedition to him." At the first streaks of the morning-light the dispersed fleet came together; no vessel had perished.*

The virtue of a just man ran an imminent risk. The world was going to be filled with the noise of a great scandal. Satan was rejoicing.

* Guillaume le Breton, Philippide, 4. Life of St Columbanus, Boll

In his prayer the religious bethought him of souls in trial : there was no fall !

A soul, a prey to despair, had resolved to put an end to her life. She was going to brave the justice she did not dream of bending. . . . What hand will stay her ? The hand that, from the depths of the cell, stretches itself out to God.

A sinner, on the point of falling into eternity, was repelling the tenderness of mercy. His angel had a hard task to gather, in a long life, what he found of good : it was little, after such a mass of crimes ! Suddenly, in the balance are thrown mortifications and fastings. Angel of the cell, still another soul who will owe her safety to you !

A mother was dying. Poor orphans ! what is to become of you ? They press around her, having no resource but their tears ; who will stop death ? who will save for them this hand to guide them, these eyes to watch over them, this heart to love them ?

20

Angels of these little ones, take their sighs and their sobs, fly to the cell, and you also will come back with consolation and with joy.

LXVI.

The Angel of the Priest.

I.

THE Levite had grown up in the shadow of the sanctuary. A high honor was reserved for him, and the family were going to receive abundant blessings.

From the moment of his birth the angels had known that he would shed great lustre around the Church. They had come to rest on the roof that covered his cradle; they had sung his baptism, and foretold his sanctity.*

* Lives of SS. Moschua, Keintegern, and Gudula, Boll.

231

The design of God was beginning to re-
veal itself. The mother of the young man
was going to understand the vision she had
once had.

The angel who was to guide her son had
appeared to her, holding a veil strewn over
with flowers. She saw this veil float off in
the distance, open out, and cover the meadows, the woods, and the mountains. " Thy
child shall flower for heaven," said the angel to her, "and souls without number will
owe to him their safety." *

On the day when he was clothed with the
priesthood and placed amid the princes of
the people of God, we saw his angel fall the
first at his feet, and kiss his hands.

Those hands that had just received a sacred character, were more resplendent than
ours. They were going too to exercise func-
tions more sublime, and scatter greater treasures. With the power to touch and bear

* Life of St Columbanus, Boll.

sacred things, they had received the virtue of making holy and of blessing things profane.

In the new priest the guardian angel saluted a superior in power and in dignity. In going out of the sanctuary he yielded the way to him with humble deference. He esteemed himself too much honored in approaching and in aiding him whom he saw become an earthly God and a second Jesus Christ; him whose word will bring down God to earth, and raise souls to heaven.*

A more perfect life was to correspond to so high a dignity : the angel redoubled his care.

The imperfections inherent to human nature, and which remained in the priest, did not discourage him: he knew they would have their use.

Subject to weakness unknown of angels, the priest will be better able to pity those of

* St Bernard, Synodal Disc. St Francis of Assisium, Opusc 22
    20 *

sinners. The angels would, perhaps, sometimes feel indignation get the better of their pity. The priest will only have to think of himself, that everything may become in him goodness and gentleness.

The keys of heaven are well placed in the hands of a man.*

II.

When the minister of J. C. mounted the chair of truth, the zeal of the angel was in his heart and animated his words. The angels of the faithful gave ear, and sent him a thousand returns of thanks.†

When he came to take his seat at the Divine tribunal, to absolve sinners and replace on their brows the crown they had lost, the angel cried in admiration: " Who but God can remit sins, and make pure that which was unclean ? " ‡

* St. Chrysostom, On St. Peter and Elias.

† St Bernard, Comm. on the Cant of Canticles   Lives of SS. Basil, Ambrose, Sebastian, Vincent Ferrer, Bernardin of Fettres, Boll

‡ Job xiv 4   St Mark ii 7   Philip the Solitary, Letter to the Monk Callirus, 3

When, a living throne, the priest had to bear in triumph the King of Heaven, and distribute to souls the manna of the Eucharist, the angel accompanied him with trembling, himself surrounded by other angels.*

When he received the infant at the entrance of life and clothed it with innocence, or when he assisted the old man at his departure from the world, and gave him strength through the holy unction, the angel was filled with joy, and celebrated these wonders.†

But when, in the presence of the heavenly court, which he flooded with his light, the priest consecrated the Body and Blood of the Saviour, and in the name of a God pronounced those words, "This is my Body; this is the chalice of my Blood," his angel, as if annihilated, bent to the earth, and did not dare raise his eyes; neither cherubim nor

* St. Nilus, Letter to Anastasius.
† St. Gregory Nazianzen, On Baptism.

seraphim had appeared to him in so elevated a position.*

III.

The angel of the priest saw in the distance the angels of nations, yet sitting in the shadow of death, turn toward him with an expression of grief, and he heard them cry: "Help us!" †

To comply with their wishes, he transmitted to the heart, whose generosity he knew, a lively image of this distress, and pressed him to devote himself to the salvation of infidels.‡

He did more: armed with a sharp arrow, he pierced this heart through, and made it feel the irresistible yearnings of zeal.§

In a few days the young priest was

---

* St. Bernard, Instructio Sacerdotalis St Chrysostom, Treatise on the Priesthood, lib 3, and Homily 83.

† Acts of the Apostles xvi 9

‡ St. Jerome, Comm on Isaiah St Nilus, Letters to Mitelius Lives of SS. Vivencian, Patrick, and Paul of Leon, Boll.

§ Life of St. Theresa, written by herself.

changed into a fervent apostle, and the angel said to him: "Come."

Around about the vessel that received them thousands of spirits came hovering, swelling the happy sails with their breath, stilling the waves, and singing: "Arise, be enlightened, O Jerusalem; for thy light is come, and the glory of the Lord is risen upon thee." *

At the sight of the countless crowns borne to souls crushed by slavery, Satan was moved. He called together his powers, bade them stop the enterprise and overwhelm it with catastrophe.

The night, the winds, the lightning, all united at his voice; all was confusion, everything was tempest. The heavens and the waters struggled with fury, and above their roaring were to be heard bursts of hellish laughter.

More than once the vessel was on the

* Isaiah lx 1.

point of being swallowed up, but guardian
arms upheld it.   Despite the demons, the
angels who direct the elements brought back
calm and serenity, and all the voyagers
chanted a hymn of deliverance.*

IV.

The moment the messenger of salvation
touched the shore, the angels of the infidel
people flew to meet him.

"Blessed be he," said they, "who cometh
in the name of the Lord! He will be our
consoler and our aid, he will open to us
hearts that were closed to us, will make us
known to those who know us not, will make
our ministry fruitful.   How many souls
snatched from Satan and carried to the
arms of their God through the ministry of
the priest and of the angel!"

At the moment the Divine Sacrifice was
offered for the first time, a heavenly light

* Life of St. Felan, Boll.

enveloped the land. The powers of darkness were agitated and made the ground tremble. Their authority had just received a mortal blow; Jesus Christ was inaugurating his reign.

A priestly hand aided by a thousand angelic hands had raised, in the heart of this empire, a ladder of the elect. At first we saw mount it some souls of little children, then some souls of aged men, then souls of every age and condition.

When the apostle directed his course through idolatrous peoples, angels led him to those who had kept the natural law, or had gone astray from it the least, and who seemed ripe for baptism or penance. Under the appearance of chance an intelligent Providence became his guide.*

" Who art thou that strivest alone against a world, and dost triumph over it?" cried the demon.

* Life of St. Columbanus, Boll.

"My name is Legion," answered the apostle, retorting against Satan the words of Satan himself. "Thou seest only me, a weak and infirm instrument; but with me are the angels of my relatives and friends, of all the souls I am come to save." *

The Devil thought he had found out the secret of a brilliant victory. He wished to strike a decisive blow at his adversaries by a persecution skilfully planned. His rage deceived him. He was going to become the executor of their designs, and was on the eve of undergoing a most ignominious defeat.

v.

The angel said to the apostle: "What happiness, if in watering with thy blood the budding root thou has planted, thou couldst give it new increase?" The apostle was ravished with joy.†

---

* St Mark v 9. Origen, Comm. on St John
† St. Augustine, Pref to the Comment. on the 40th Ps Tertullian, Apologetic 50. St Epiph l. 2, cont Hæret

At the hour marked in the Divine decrees for the beginnings of the sacrifice, he was seized and thrown into a dungeon.

The admiration of the angel knew no bounds; he could not venerate sufficiently the chain that bound his limbs. Borne for Jesus Christ, it seemed more brilliant than gold; in his eyes it was a bond of honor, a splendid ornament, an incomparable livery of love: he would have wished to have given his wings for it.*

It would have been easy for him, as for the angels that freed the saints, to burst these bonds and unbar those doors. He preferred seeing hours fruitful in merit and glory flow on in this captivity. He sounded the depths of the wounds, measured the intensity of thirst and of hunger, followed with an attentive eye the progress of the sufferings.†

* St Chrys , Comm on Ep to the Ephesians. Life of St Felix of Nola, of St Julian of Mans, St Restituta, St Mayeul, Boll.

† Lives of SS. Victor, Eleutherius of Tournai, Alexander Pope, Boll

He multiplied consolations to keep up the courage of his hero. He lit up the dungeon with rays that made its walls transparent, and bathed it with perfumes unknown to the flowers of earth. He sang, accompanying himself with the sound of his vibrating wings, and produced a harmony that saved from all depression the soul in its trial.*

When the confessor repeated the psalms of bondage and of sorrow, the angels replied with those of deliverance and rejoicing.†

On the vigil of his immolation the priest felt an unbounded regret. He would have wished to offer once more the holy Victim, and fortify himself with the bread of the strong; but he lay on the bare earth, motionless, his hands tied, and he had neither matter nor altar for the sacrifice.

The angel heaped on him the wondrous favors wrought for other friends of God. In

* Lives of SS. Fursey, Vincent of Saragossa, Romanus, Lawrence, Vitus, and Theopompus, Boll.

† Lives of St. Theogenes, of St. Anastasius Mogundatus, Boll.

the midst of a globe of light he appeared to him holding a Host white as snow, and wine in a cup of gold.*

" The altar, where is the altar ? " asked the priest. " 'T is there," said the angel ; " it is ready, it glows with diamonds and rubies ; Jesus himself has chosen it. What altar is richer than a breast adorned with blood and wounds ! "

The angel placed the bread and the wine on the breast of the confessor. The latter pronounced the sacred words, received from the hands of the angel the bread of life and the chalice of salvation, then added: †

" 'T is my turn to be ground like wheat, that I may become bread worthy of Jesus Christ! Happy and a thousand times blessed be the hand that will separate me from this world to unite me to Jesus! It will be stained with guilt while it gives me happi-

* Life of St. Clement of Ancyra, Boll.
† Life of St. Lucian, priest of Antioch, of St. Zozimus, Boll.

ness; but I will pray so ardently the God of mercy that He will grant me to be able to kiss it one day in heaven." *

VI.

In the heights where the stars are sown, clouds of pure spirits appeared. They had their eyes fixed on that isle, till now obscure, which had just grown brilliant. A Calvary was ready. All heaven descended to it.†

The angel sustained the confessor and held his crown. The martyrs in triumph bent their palms toward him, in token of brotherhood; and Jesus in the midst of them opened his bosom to receive him.‡

As the blood gushed forth an infinity of hands caught the drops. They formed with them a treasure that shall be the wealth of

* Life of St Ignatius of Antioch, Boll.

† Life of St Columbanus, Boll

‡ Lives of SS Julian, Andrew Salus, Timothy, Maura, Boll , of St Tryphon, and Respicius, Dom Raynard

a parricidal people. That blood as a shower of graces and blessings will fall upon souls to convert and save them: 'T is thus the martyr revenges himself.*

At the last sigh a flash darted from the clouds and went down into the abyss. Satan had been dethroned. The rod of iron had flown into pieces. The people so long crushed by an accursed foot, were now about to breathe. Like a wonderful oil, the blood had increased a hundred-fold the fire of Divine love in the hearts of men.†

The angels were heard singing a song of triumph: " Who is he that cometh clad in raiment of purple, glorious with shining wounds? How beautiful is this soldier who has conquered hell, has given a kingdom to his prince, and who has come laden with spoils! The Church the apostle has founded

* St Augustine, On the Sermon on the Mount, lib. 1
† Idem, Comm on Ps 4.

21 *

is worthy of her mother; she bears the seal of sacrifice and of immolation.*

And other angels who surrounded the martyr added:

"Lift up, O ye princes of heaven, the gates of the eternal city! The new conqueror will make his victories serve to build up the Jerusalem above. The empty places in your ranks shall be filled up. To wicked spirits will succeed in love the souls converted by the zeal of the priest." †

Laments were mingled with the hymns and songs:

"Why have you not given us, too, a body? Why shall man alone enjoy the happiness of dying for you?" ‡

But a voice answered these words: "'T is for man that a God died; — it becomes man to die for his God!" §

---

* Isaias lxiii. St Ephraim, Eulogium of the Martyrs. St. Cyprian, Exhort. to Martyrs

† Ps 23.　　　‡ Michel Vivien, Tertullianus prædicans.

§ St. Asterus, Eulogium of the Martyr St. Phocas, Tertul de Resur 8

A thousand leagues from this Calvary a prodigy filled hearts with emotion.

At the paternal fireside had remained hanging, silent and mute since his departure, the guitar on which the future martyr accompanied himself as he charmed the family with holy canticles. This guitar began of itself to sound with sweet notes, accompanying a heavenly voice that said:

"Happy are the saints who have followed the footsteps of the Lamb! Their souls rejoice in the sacred precincts. And because they have shed their blood for Jesus Christ, they will reign eternally in his glory." *

VII.

In his diadem the priest could count as many jewels as he had saved souls. These souls hailed him with joyous acclamations:

"Glory to the apostle, to the confessor, to the pastor, to the martyr!" †

* Life of St. Dunstan, Boll
† Life of St. William, Ab, Boll.

While he was receiving his crown in the bosom of God, his memory and his remains were having on earth the honors that only the Church can dispense.

Love had broken the vase of perfumes upon the feet of the Master, and the perfumes had been spread around. The precious fragments were to be gathered, to continue giving forth their sweetness for ages to come.*

The tyrant who had just given heaven to the martyr, would have wished to refuse him the earth. He ordered the body to be carried far out to sea, to be buried in the waves.

It was seen on the horizon like to a sun that rises from the waves and darts his first rays. Angels brought it back to the shore, fanning it with their wings, and chanting the victory of which it had been the instrument.†

* St Paschasius Radbertus, Comm on St Matthew
† St Theodore Studite, Discourse on the Assembly of the Heavenly Hosts Lives of SS Clement of Ancyra, Agathangelus, Thyrsus, Andéol, Julian, Pr, Boll

Enlightened by this homage, men came in their turn to honor the august relic. It spread around a heavenly virtue that inspired holiness, and wrought miracles.

The tomb that covered it soon became glorious. It was seen to rise, grow larger, extend and transform itself into a vast church, which will remain, under the name of the martyr.

His holy relics lie under the altar of sacrifice. Each day, through all time, the Saviour will come to immolate himself on the body of his priest immolated for his God.

The martyr will live in the memory of his neophytes. They will tell his history to their children, and give them his name. They will teach them to pray to him, to bless him, to celebrate his triumph each year. To the latest posterity the remembrance of him shall be full of love.*

* Eccl xliv.

LXVII.

The Angel of the Mother.

EAKENED by age, and seeing her end near, the mother blessed God for His favors granted her in her children. The angel called together about her the angels of the family, and asked them what had been the joys of their ministry. Each one answered by praising his charge.

The angel of the little chosen one unfolded the robe of innocence; the virgin's showed the brilliant roses of Divine love; the soldier's held up the banner nobly defended; that of the religious spoke of heaven on earth; the priest pointed with his hand to the altar of consecration, to the ladder of salvation, to the dungeon, to the Calvary.

"Thanks, well-beloved brothers," said to them with a sweet smile the angel of the mother. "These are my treasures you have just displayed. How weave for the mother a crown of glory without taking for it some rays of beauty from those of her children? Is she not the stem upon which they have flourished, and did they not receive from her the first perfume of their holiness? *

"She promised them to God before their birth, consecrated them to Him on the day of their baptism, and never after ceased renewing an offering dear to her faith.†

"I have seen her rejoicing in their joy, suffering in their sorrow, weeping with their tears, living more in them than in herself.

"'T was thus she prepared them for the

---

* St Theresa, On Foundations, ch. xx.
† Life of St Gregory Naz., Boll

sacrifices you caused them to make, and she had to share. She was the free instrument of grace to bring about the acts you were ravished in beholding.*

" How sweet it is to me, my well-beloved brothers, to hear you celebrate the glory of the mother of the family? Soon I will invoke your testimony before God. When I shall be asked about her life, I shall let the angels of her children speak. Her children and their virtues will be the precious stones and jewels with which she will be decked on entering heaven.†

" This angel was the one I loved most, and who most loved me. He found in me the angel of Jacob, and I saw in him the angel of Rachel."

* St. Peter Damian, Serm 17
† St Jerome, Letter to Eustochium.

LXVIII.

The Angel of the Servant.

THROUGH the coarse garments of the good servant his angel showed us the supernatural brightness his soul shed around. Pure and beautiful was the virtue that adorned it, but it had not been gained without effort.

In the secret of his heart, Satan said to him one day: "Why are these the masters, and you only a servant?" "And why in the body are the eyes the eyes, and the hands only the hands?" replied at once this simple man, inspired by his angel.

Satan wished to make him fail in his trust.
"You are alone," said he; "no one sees you,
no one will be able to suspect you." "And
the Eye that watches from the depth of eternity, since when has it grown darkened?"
answered once more the angel by the voice
of the servant.

Satan, seeing his unshaken virtue, tried to
fill him with vanity.   With perfidious voice
he said to him :

"You are humble, pious, docile, faithful
in everything. There are few servants as
perfect as you.   You have been leading a
holy life for a long time.   I am an angel
sent by God to congratulate you on your
victories over the Evil One, and to show you
the greatness of your merits." *

To warn him of the snare, the guardian
angel presented to the mind of the servant a
mirror, in which were united all the infideli-

* Paralipomena of SS. Pacomius and Theodore.   St John Climacus, Scala Cœli

ties of his life, and all the imperfections he still had. The servant was horror-stricken at the sight of himself, and hastened to say to the unmasked deceiver:

"They have played with you, beautiful angel. The magnificent description they have given you is not of me. For my part, I am only a miserable sinner." * Satan had fled, and the good servant received from his angel a pledge of the warmest affection.

Caring little for worldly acquaintances from whom his position kept him aloof, he had made astonishing progress in the science of salvation. With his angel for his master, and his crucifix for his book, he had acquired the practice of solid virtues.

'Twas from this school and from this book that he drew his last consolation. When death came, it found him giving ear to his angel, and with his head bent over the image of Jesus on the cross.

* Book of the Doctrine of the Holy Fathers.

Never had a wealthy, thoughtless man at his funeral so noble a cortege. The carriage was surrounded by angels, who repeated the Divine words:

" Well done, good servant! Because thou hast been faithful over a few things, I will intrust to thee many things. Enter into the joy of thy Lord." *

* St. Matthew v. 11. St. Chrysologus, Serm. 115. Life of St. Raygnier, Boll.

LXIX.

The Higher Angels.

OUR ministry as guardian angels had in no wise suspended our relations with our brothers in heaven. On the contrary they have been rendered more frequent. We were obliged to have recourse to their mediation, not for ourselves, but for the souls we were guiding.*

In that vast hierarchy God forms among the spirits, grace is transmitted from the highest to those beneath them. The Re-

* St. Dionysius, De Cœlest. Hier., iii. iv. St. Thomas, De Angelis, q. 107, 111.

deemer is the principle of it. It flows from
His breast to the heart of Mary — comes
down through the Seraphim, the Cherubim,
the Thrones, the Dominations, the Virtues,
the Powers, the Principalities, the Archangels, the Angels — until it reaches man.*

All is bound together in this sublime con-
trolling agency; and it is in this way we
form the living providence of God.

Men ponder with admiration the source
whence grace flows, and behold its beauty,
life, and saving influence burst forth. But
do they dream of the brilliant channel
through which these fertilizing waters come
to them?

What enchanting joy for the father of the
family the day he saw that immense chain,
the first link of which was in the heart of
God, and the last in the hand his good
angel stretched out to him! †

*Nicetas Choniates. Treasure of the True Faith, b. 2, c. lx
† St. Hilary, Comm on Ps 118.

Without these relations of earth with heaven, what would become of man?

To get hold of the souls he besets, the demon would not have need of violent attacks. Barrenness and famine would soon give them up to him.

To banish the angels from this lower world would be to strip it of its glory and of its ornaments. Instead of shining with light and life, it would have for its part only darkness and death. Men would give up those magnificent heights where pure spirits preside, and would dream only of burying themselves in the depths of matter.*

Without the angels this world here below would have neither poetry, nor grandeur, nor anywhere in it could hope be hailed. Well does he know it who sows everywhere the seeds of rationalism that so great a number

* St Clement of Alexandria, Stromata, 4   St. Ambrose, Comm on St Luke

of souls take in. He does not destroy spiritual and supernatural realities, but he veils the view of them, and keeps hearts from lifting themselves to their level.

LXX.

The Divine Countenance.

OUR duties did not withdraw us from the Divine Countenance. We had it ever present to us, and in its light all that exists was seen.*

Our movements were made in the bosom of God. Through the brilliant regions of infinite space we mounted, we descended, we directed our untrammelled flight.

Our country filled us with its charms even in the midst of the exile in which we followed our friends.

* St. Matthew xviii. 10. St. Gregory the Great, Moralia, 2. St. Thomas, De Angelis, quæst. 112, art. 3.

261

No distance dimmed our sight, no obstacle hindered it, no shadow troubled it, no multiplicity of objects distracted it, no combination of things absorbed it, no detail escaped it.

There is no tiny worm of the earth, no grain of sand, no drop of dew, whose destiny is not as well known to us as that of worlds.

And, in like manner, heaven offers us no palm, no crown, no jewel, the history of which has not had us for witnesses, and which is not a touching token for us.

The care we give to a soul does not keep us from hearing the harmony of angels, and taking part in it, from assisting at the triumph of the just and applauding it, from seeing the prayers of men ascend, and from admiring the distribution of graces.

Heaven, earth, hell, are unfolded before us. For us struggle, chastisement, reward, have no secret. The Divine Countenance spreads over all creation a clearness that nothing can veil from our eyes.

In their present state, men find it hard to conceive this privilege. Only glory can give the force and strength of spirit necessary for the clear and simultaneous view of things.

LXXI.

Old Age.

WHILE each member of the family was following the way in which he had been called by God, and was fulfilling his destiny, a void began to be made around its head. The companions of his childhood had disappeared. He was there like the relic of a past age.

One friend, however, kept by him, a very old friend, though full of youth, the one God had given him at his entry into life, who watched over his cradle, and was present every moment of his career in life.

"My friendship," said he, addressing the

soul, "has not grown cold on account of the ravages of time undergone by the body. Infirmity and age have not been able to affect it." The soul of the old man was as vigorous and as healthy as on the first day. I saw in her an eye more pure, an ear as delicate, as serene a brow, as tender a heart.

My interest had grown on account of the care I had lavished upon him. The more this soul had cost me, the dearer she was to me. I did not wish to have done her in vain so many acts of generosity. Is it not when the bee has hovered longest around the flowers that he has most love for his treasure ?*

I fortified the friend of God against discouragement and melancholy. When the earth grew sombre and showed him only things that were perishable, I made him see the splendors of heaven, and fixed his thoughts on things that do not pass away.

* St. Thomas of Villanova, On the Angels.

23

My presence dissipated the shadows around him, and consoled him in his moments of weakness. It took the place, for him, of relations and friends; I, alone even, was for him the whole world. I could not think of his near entry into glory without lively joy. I had not to wait long before seeing his last hour. A long life is so great a good for those who pass it in the friendship of God! It is by a long life that a virtuous soul can increase indefinitely her merits and raise herself above the angels. The angels had but one moment to merit.*

* St. Thomas, De Angelis, quæst. 62, art. 5.

LXXII.

The Illness.

GOD wished to purify him by a last sacrifice, to make him gain a more beautiful reward. Sickness came upon him.

I never left his pillow. My place was near the pyre upon which were to be burned the remains of his imperfections.

While I was urging him to unite his sufferings with those of his Saviour, he saw, in spirit, angels descending from heaven and ranging themselves around his bed. One held in his hands the cross, another the lance, a third the nails, a fourth the thorns, a fifth the reed, one other the column, and another the chains.*

At the sight of these instruments, borne with respect by angels, he felt a lively impression of the Divine sufferings, and aspired on his part only to undergo his passion.

Without lessening the price of his holocaust I tempered the bitterness of the cup.

"Courage!" I said to him; "thanks to infirmity and sickness, your body is going to fall into dust. 'T is the wall raised between you and your country that is shaken and falls down. Will you complain if the passage through the breach gives you some moments of trial? Happy pilot, will you choose the hour of entering port to give yourself to sadness? Is it not rather the time to dry your tears, and give forth a chant of joy?"

These thoughts were so gently insinuated into his heart that they seemed to well up

* Life of St. Lidwina, Boll

of themselves, and he took them for his own.

I became in this way the instrument of Divine mercy, to soften the hard couch upon which he lay. My compassión and solicitude redoubled and grew with his pains.*

* Ps. xl. 4.   St. Pantaleo, Discourse on St. Michael.

23 *

LXXIII.

The Tidings of Departure.

ONE night, as I was engaged in consoling him, I perceived, in the house of God, angels who were strewing, on the pavement of the sanctuary, violets, lilies, and roses.

"What are you doing, my blessed brethren?" I asked them; "and what does this spectacle mean?"

"We shall soon have a feast here," they answered, "and we are making the preparations."*

I understood for whom this feast was in

* Life of B. Robert, Cistercian.

reserve, and what part I was to take in it. It was to be celebrated in the midst of the tears of earth and the joys of heaven.

The moment had come to do a favor to the old man, that God reserves for His most intimate friends.

Up to this the uncertainty regarding the term of his career had been a benefit. It had stimulated him to vigilance and fervor. He sanctified each day of his life, when each one might be the last

But on the eve of his departure certainty became a grace.

In fixing his thoughts on a point sure and so near, what would not be the result? what detachment from all that is earthly! what elevation of thought, what regret for faults, what darts of love!

I revealed to him the day and the hour when he would burst the bonds of his captivity. "I rejoice," he cried, "at the words

that are said to me: we shall enter into the
house of the Lord."*

* Ps. cxxi.   Lives of SS. Meneleus, Stephen Sabaite, Paul of Leon,
Cedd., Boll.

LXXIV.

The Supplication.

SINCE he had no longer facility of speaking to God, it was my duty to speak for him. While still full of vigor and in the strength of youth, he had placed in my heart this supplication:

"My good Angel!

"I know not when nor how I shall die. It is possible I may be carried off suddenly, and that before my last sigh I may be deprived of all intelligence. Yet how many things I should wish to say to God on the threshold of eternity!

"In the full freedom of my will, to-day, I

come to charge you to speak for me at that fearful moment. You will say to Him then, O my good angel:

"That I wish to die in the Catholic, Apostolic Roman Church, in which all the saints since Jesus Christ have died, and out of which there is no salvation:

"That I ask the grace of sharing in the infinite merits of my Redeemer, and that I desire to die in pressing to my lips the cross that was bathed in His blood:

"That I detest my sins because they displease Him; and that I pardon, through love of Him, all my enemies, as I wish myself to be pardoned:

"That I die willingly because He orders it, and that I throw myself with confidence into His adorable heart, awaiting all His mercy:

"That in my inexpressible desire to go to heaven, I am disposed to suffer everything it may please His sovereign justice to inflict on me:

"That I love Him before all things, above all things, and for His own sake; that I wish and hope to love Him with the elect, His angels, and the blessed Mary, during all eternity.

"Do not refuse, O my angel, to be my interpreter with God, and to protest to Him that these are my sentiments, and my will." *

My heart and my voice went together in repeating to God, at the stated time, this beautiful protest. God accepted it as if it had come that moment from the soul of the dying man.

* St. Ch. Borromeo, Supp. to his Angel Guardian.

LXXV.

The Last Assault.

 ATAN, seeing his struggle with me about to commence, showed a desperate obstinacy.* What difference did it make to him to have been up to that time defeated and covered with shame? If he had been able to gain in this last combat, would he not have been consoled for his former failures?

Not having been able to strand the vessel when it was passing through dangerous straits, and was sailing between the reefs of

---

* J. Lopes, Abridgment of the Teaching of the Holy Fathers.

the coast and the fury of the high seas, he came to await it at the port.*

At his voice legions of dark spirits ran to aid him. He gave the preference to those who had most tormented the good Christian during his life. They would know best with whom they had to deal.†

"Recall," he said to them, "the faults into which you made him fall. Exaggerate them in his sight as much as you formerly lessened them. Transform into a crime what you before suggested as harmless. Crush him under the weight of these sad memories. Already oppressed by disease, he will not be able to offer a long resistance. Discouragement and despair—these are your arms; if they do not gain us the victory, all is lost! Go, then, and outdo yourselves. Whoever will ruin him shall have the satisfaction of tormenting him in hell." ‡

---

* St J. Chrysost. Comm on the Text, Vidi Dominum.

† J. Lopes, Op. cit

‡ St Thomas, On the Angels, q 113, art. 4.

24

Just as vile vultures, in rapid flight, pass over the clear streams, the smiling plains, the golden harvests, to go light, in an infectious marsh, on some unclean prey, so the demons, going through the extent of this beautiful life, shut their eyes to the good due to the energy of virtue, and gathered only the evil that had been the result of weakness.*

Thoughts of discouragement beset the dying man. He, who had led a holy life, after some faults immediately wept over, heard day and night threatening voices: "Woe to thee, accursed; not one sin has been remitted thee!"

* St. Basil of Cæsarea, Homily on Envy.

LXXVI.

Reassurance.

IN the midst of darkness I re-assured the just man:

"Let the demons roar; continue to hope. For whom are those sufferings and that death of the Redeemer, if not for those who with faith claim the aid of them, and apply to themselves their effects? Do you think that He will, with that hand pierced for love of you, repel you from that heart in like manner pierced for love of you?* The remembrance of your faults should humble you, not make you lose cour-

---

* Jean Lopes, Abridgment of the Teaching of the Holy Fathers.

279

age. You placed them in the bosom of mercy, and you can rely on the indulgence of a God, the friend of hearts that repent. If you fear you have not been severe enough in your self-accusations, look again into the secrets of your conscience, and the last absolution will remove at a touch the last stains.

"You regret not having sufficiently expiated faults that have been pardoned? Penance comes to you of its own accord; behold it in the pains you suffer. It is the choice of your Saviour, and is worth much more than what you would choose. Suffer and hope; and hope because you suffer."

He fixed his gaze on the wounds of Jesus, and heard the voice that knew how to say to a life-long friend, better even than to the friend of a moment: " This day thou shalt be with me in paradise." *

'T was in this way I fixed him to the chain which hangs from heaven toward the elect,

* St. Luke xxiii. 43.

and which is called hope. Holding to it strongly, he was bold enough to say to the tempter : *

"In vain, cruel beast, you come to lay snares for my soul. It belongs to you by no title. You will find nothing in me, on which your malice can lay hold. I belong to God, to His mercy, to His love; in this I am, and in this I shall be for all eternity !" †

* St. Chrysost., To Theodorus.
† Life of St. Martin of Tours. Sulp. Severus.

24 *

LXXVII.

Extreme Unction.

THE dying Christian was an athlete fighting his last combat. To make him equal to the undertaking, the Church conferred on him extreme unction.

The priest said, on entering, "Peace to this house and to all who dwell in it. May wicked spirits depart, may good angels come, and may the guardian of this house drive from it all fear and troubles." *

By the imposition of hands made in the name of the Father, of the Son, and of the

---

* Ceremonies of Extreme Unction.

Holy Ghost, the minister of Divine consolations drives off the influence of Satan. He then invokes the angels, archangels, patriarchs, prophets, apostles, martyrs, confessors, and virgins, and places the sick man under their protection.

The guardian angel of this house, at the same time that of its head, calls together the angels of the family. They come with gladness to this roof, which was the asylum of such beautiful virtues. They bring with them, in the name of the children, precious aid for the dying man.

Upon each organ, and upon each sense, is traced the sign of the cross. The power of this sign destroys the last vestiges of sins committed by sight, hearing, smell, taste, speech, touch, and motion.

We admired, in this work, the sweetness of mercy. It did not cease to surprise us by the variety and efficacy of its means. It was inexhaustible in resources, and adapted them to each want of the soul. In putting together its treasures, it had in view the complete reunion of human weaknesses.

The cross was to the demons as a rampart that covered the just man, and allowed him to brave them; or like the sword, which through the angels gave them bloody wounds; or like an invulnerable hammer that crushed their serpents' heads, or like a net in which they were taken, believing they would ensnare the God-man by it.*

They continued to roar, but their roaring only expressed impotence. Audacious as they were before, they were now as timid. They had commenced to tremble, from the time they had seen this soul gain new strength, and in his turn threaten them. Bold before cowards, they will always be cowards before the brave.†

* St. Chrysost., On St. Matthew. Life of Blessed Bagnesia, Boll.
† Ps. lxxxviii

LXXVIII.

The Viaticum.

NOT content with having placed the dying man beyond the reach of Satan, the Redeemer wished himself to be his strength and defence.

He whom we have seen become the God of innocence, the God of the sinner, the God of the penitent, the God of the just man, put the finishing stroke to His goodness in making himself the God of the dying Christian.

Accompanied by angels, who bore their torches, He quitted his tabernacle, went out of the temple, traversed the streets, pene-

trated into the by-ways, betook himself to
the humble dwelling, and visited the friend
from whom He had first received such cordial visits.*

From the look he gave him, he seemed
to us sweet as love, tender as compassion itself, indulgent as mercy. In the presence
of the princes of heaven who formed his
Eucharistic Court, he manifested his love
for a man lost in the obscurity of a simple
life.

He did not offer him only the aid of his
ministers or the succor of his arm ; he said
to him :

"Open to me thy heart; 't is in the bosom
of thy body and of thy soul I wish to place
myself. Thou shalt not depart without me,
but with me thou shalt go without fear.
Whoever rises up against thee will soon find
he has to do with a God."

The Divine Viaticum gave the traveller

* Life of St Veronica de Binasco, Boll.

light, patience, courage, all he could desire, all his enemies could fear.

The devils dreamed no longer of coming near him. In that breast they felt was hidden their ruler and their judge. They saw themselves disarmed, and acknowledged themselves vanquished.*

I rejoiced in their dismay, and in the confidence of the old man: "What do you fear?" I said to him; "you bear in your body the Master of life and of death, the King of time and of eternity."

* St. J. Chrysostom, Comm. on the 41st Ps. Homily 61. Life of St. Mucarius, Boll.

LXXIX.

The Departure.

A T last the soul had to depart. "You who loved her, remain there! You cannot follow her with your look, and know what way she takes. She will not be able on her part to send you any token of joy or of sorrow. Oh, solitude! Oh, frightful isolation!"

But no! solitude and isolation were only imaginary. This soul was not condemned to cross alone and unguided the fearful threshold.

A companion was with him, that of his

whole life, he who had aided him in taking so many difficult steps.*

"Give me thy hand, soul dear to me as a sister. 'T is not to-day thy guardian angel, who was so devoted to thee, will abandon thee. I know the way thou art about to take : I have gone over it so often when taking thy prayers to God, and bringing back from God His graces." †

I was yet speaking. . . . "Silence!" cried all at once the dying man; "do you not hear that harmony and those chants ? "

The assistants were still ; they listen, they see the feeble hands strive to raise themselves to heaven, they hear him murmur :

" I salute you, O my guardian angel, and I wish you the good day of eternity! I salute you, O Mary, my mother ; O Jesus, my Redeemer ; O ye blessed elect, who form the

---

* St. Bernard, On Ps. xc.

† Tobias v 7, 8. St. Thomas of Villanova, On the Angels. St Bernard, Comm. on the Cant. of Canticles.

crown of my God.   I salute you, and wish you the good day of eternity." *

There his words ceased, but his look seemed to follow an apparition.†

They approach him with religious respect, they admire the calm of his features, the smile of his lips, the supernatural beauty of his countenance.   They are afraid of disturbing his extasy, they scarcely dare draw breath, they wait . . . . And he too waits, but upon another shore.   Gliding lightly from the dust that clothed her, his soul has taken her flight to the pure spirits.

* Lives of SS. Servulus, Veronica, Boll ; of St. Redempta.
† St Gregory the Great, Dialogues.   Death of Louis XVII , de Beau Chère.

LXXX.

The Arrival.

THE last breath drawn, and the veil rent, where did the soul of the old man see herself? In the arms of her angel. For the first time I appeared to her as I am, and I gave her the fraternal embrace.

How sweet was my presence to her! My holiness, my greatness, my power with God, all was consolation for her. She saw herself more than indissolubly united to me.

From our very first steps into eternity we saw ourselves surrounded by joyful choirs who wished us welcome, in congratulating us

291

on our victories. They closed their brilliant circles around us, waked to life their harps, and spread around a light that enveloped us in a common aureola.*

The apostles bore on their foreheads that royal majesty which will strike the eyes of all at the last day, when, as an august senate, they will sit with Jesus Christ to judge the universe.†

The martyrs came forward as an army of conquerors, distinguished by garments whiter than snow, and by wounds more resplendent than the sun.

The confessors reproduced in the shades of their beauty, the infinite variety of their virtues, and were alike in that perfect purity marked by the lilies with which they were crowned.

The virgins applauded with their hands,

* Prayers for the Recommendation of a Soul. Lives of SS. Ermitus Infant, Germanus of Capua, Aidanus, Pourçain, Stephen of Grammont, Louis of Toulouse, Boll.

† Prayers for the Recommendation of a Soul.

and cried out for joy, and sang again the canticle of the Lamb, at the sight of a soul saved by His blood.

At the head of the heavenly legions was the Archangel Michael, chief of the armies of God, and the great conductor of just souls into eternity. He bore in one hand the sword of flame, and in the other the standard of Divine victories.

Received at the entrance of the invisible world by this beautiful cortege, we had not to pass through any region of darkness. No snare, no enemy was met with on the road. Satan and his satellites, after having observed from a distance the events of our agony, had fled, saying, "One more soul who will enjoy glory inaccessible to demons." *

* Prayers for the Recommendation of a Soul

25 *

LXXXI.

The Judgment.

I PRESENTED the soul to the Judge. He held out his hand to her: "Well-beloved soul, fear not. Recognize the Master thou hast served faithfully, and whom thou hast made thy debtor. Thou didst prefer me to everything, in time, shall I be able to disown thee in eternity?"

"I love Thee, my good Saviour!" cried the soul, rushing to the embrace of Jesus.*

Docile to my teachings, she had made her Judge her best friend. She had not to fear

* St. Augustine, Conference with Maximin. St. Thomas Villanova, On the Angels. Godfrey, Abbot, Homilies.

294

any rigor on his part. The Redeemer does not allow himself to be outdone in generosity.

The demon appeared nevertheless, not to destroy a soul already in possession of salvation, but to render her justification more imposing. It was proper that the impostor should be once more overwhelmed with confusion. He opened the book of death. What pleasure to be the accuser of the very faults he had caused to be committed! He did not see that those faults, once washed out, could not become matter of condemnation.*

I opened the book of life. The name of this soul shone there in immortal characters. His virtues and his works had been carefully inscribed in it. His faults were seen there only through the Divine blood that paid the ransom for them. The remembrance of them

* St. Hilary, Comm on Ps. cxviii. Raoul Ardent, On the Angels. Lives of SS Antoninus, Viventian, Veronica, Felix Capucin, Mary of Antioch, Boll.

is preserved only to make shine forth the divine mercy, of which they were the object. The Judge recalled them only to confirm their pardon.*

The scales were brought. On the side of the good actions I put the treasure of her virtues; in vain did Satan throw into the opposite side the deeds of evil. The good in all its value gained; the evil remitted had never had any weight.†

Happy to give full scope to my zeal, I did not confine myself to repelling unjust accusations; I exalted the virtues of my client, and showed how great ought to be the recompense. Fully devoted to her interests, which I looked on as my own, and knowing the indulgence and goodness of her Judge, I poured out my heart in my discourse.‡

There was no need of my enlightening

* Life of St John of Pulsano, Boll
† Life of St Elizabeth of Sconauge, Boll
‡ John Lopes, Abridg of the Teaching of the Holy Fathers Boudon, Devotion to the Nine Choirs of Angels

Him, who is light by essence, nor of inspiring favorable sentiments in One who is the source of all love; but He himself wished to reserve to me the honor and joy of obtaining for a soul I cherished an increase of glory.

The sentence was pronounced, a sentence of benediction, that gave to heaven one more of the elect, and brought to my bosom an overflow of happiness.

LXXXII.

Purgatory.

SPOT had been discerned by the eye of God. One must be pure to present himself before infinite purity. The just soul could not reach His throne, except by going through the place of expiation. I led her thither. We read sculptured over the entrance this consoling inscription : *

"THE SOJOURN OF HOPE!"

Sure of eternal glory and consumed by charity, she received without terror the pains that were inflicted on her.

* Life of St. Frances of Rome, Boll.

Of her own accord and with desire she plunged into the crucible.

Could she have done so, she would not have wished to enjoy the full vision without having first satisfied sovereign justice.*

The flames of purgatory are not dark like those of hell; they are clear and brilliant. Their brightness yields only to that of the souls that dwell in them. They cause, however, sharp suffering, and I was obliged to moderate their activity.†

The wicked spirit who had assisted at the judgment as accuser, followed us to the brink. There he stopped, and began to rail at the soul for the faults she was expiating. ‡

I strove against the effects of this horrible sight, showing myself frequently, and multiplying the tokens of my friendship. §

By secret inspirations I urged the living

---

* Louis de Blois, Retreat of the Faithful Soul. Life of St. Gertrude, Boll.

† Life of St. Frances of Rome, Boll

‡ Life of St. Margaret of Cortona, Boll.

§ J Marchant, Garden of Pastors. Boudon, Devotion to the Nine Choirs of Angels

to remember the captive soul. The angels of the family re-echoed my voice, and gained the aid of prayers and of alms. The angels of heaven answered my supplications, by inviting souls, once in like manner comforted, to repay their debt of gratitude.

So much suffrage opened the spring of the Precious Blood. I poured it upon her like a refreshing dew.*

The soul was to suffer a yet longer time, when those flames were suddenly extinguished.

In the cup I was pouring out there had been thrown some drops of an expiating blood. Whence came this blood? It had been gathered afar off, on the summit of a Calvary, and under the iron of an instrument of death: it was the blood of a martyr.

Return to thy source, O generous blood! and may the father, so worthy of the name, be freed by the supernatural merits of His glorious son.

* Life of St Catherine of Bologna, Boll

LXXXIII.

The Triumph.

A S she came out of the flames, I received the purified soul and showed her heaven.

The blessed came to meet us.*

One angel could hold in his hand all the worlds united. To bring one soul the Lord sent thousands of them. He wished to exalt and honor her in her assumption.

Each one was eager to touch the noble burden.†

Many souls that owed their salvation to

* St. Thomas of Villanova, On the Angels.
† St. Chrysostom, Homily on the Rich Man.

the prayers or examples of this new victor
gave her their thanks and threw their crowns
at her feet.

One of them broke out into magnificent
manifestations of gratitude — she who owed
her the happiness of having made a good
first communion. She had learned, on entering heaven, that without that benefit she
would have lived in sin, and been lost.

But whose are those arms that encircle the
old man, those accents that pierce him, those
hearts pressed to his heart?

He has no difficulty in recognizing them:

"O my child! O my martyr!" "Glory
to you, dearly beloved father! father of the
martyr and of the infant child!"

What happiness in the bosom of God for
the members of one family!

And what consolation for me to intro-
duce at last into eternal repose, and among
those she had loved, a soul I had so long

guided through the temptations and dangers of life !

After having made it my delight to share in her tears, how sweet it was to take part in her joy ! *

* St. Thomas of Villanova, On the Angels.

LXXXIV.

The Fallen Angel.

THE throne she was to occupy was originally destined for an angel. This angel having excluded himself from it, in the day of trial, we bestowed on the soul that received his birthright the love we should have had for him.

He would have sung the canticle of preservation; she will chant the hymn of deliverance. The concert of voices will not be the less complete — it will be more varied.*

Now, the very spirit excluded from this

* St. Thomas, De Angelis, quæst. 108, art. 8. St. Bernard, Comm. on the Canticle of Canticles.

throne was the one that had so persecuted this soul, keeping to her as if he were her shadow, and making unheard-of efforts to ruin her.

She escaped from him at last. He saw her forever withdraw from his temptations. She going to reign in glory, while he was to be thrust back into the abyss; and between the abyss and glory there was an impassable chaos.

At this last spectacle the sword of envy was turned violently in his wounds, and the apostate felt pains he himself never would have imagined.*

The last accents of heaven that sounded in his ear were the words I addressed him:

"Yes, miserable wretch; we have triumphed over thy malice, and the victory we have won is without any gain to thee!

"The Lord hath lowered himself; he took the obscure grain of dust, he hath placed it

* Life of St. Aldegoudi, Boll.

in the place of the star, and the grain of dust hath shone, it hath given light, it hath become Lucifer.

"As for thee, fallen star, thou shalt announce the day no longer. Darkness shall be thy garment and thy habitation. Thou shalt give only night, and thy name shall be Noctifer.*

"Salute, then, on the brow of this soul, the crown merited by humble wisdom; and go receive, in the depths of hell, the confusion reserved to proud folly."

* Peter de Blois, Discourse on St. Michael.

LXXXV.

The First Look.

UNANIMOUS applause greeted our arrival, and was prolonged especially in the choir amid which the soul was to have her place. She sat beside me.

Angels and souls congratulated her on her exaltation. Those who were superior to her bent down to her, through love of her, and those who were inferior to her showed themselves happy to see her so honored.

What were her impressions at this first glance she took around her in the infinite? She seemed to wish to sound its depths, sought to discover what other riches heaven possessed, and found everywhere new secrets.*

What ravishing joy at the apparition of this glorious world, in which the choirs and hierarchies are distributed with so much variety! Heaven is to her eyes a rose of vast size, of which the elect are the leaves, the Redeemer the stem, and God the life.

What transports to see hasten to her those she had known and loved during her pilgrimage, those who had been united to her by ties of blood or of friendship!

What emotion on reaching the feet of that incomparable Queen, so raised above all by her dignity and by her glory, but so near to each one by her condescension and goodness!

What extasy when the soul is penetrated by the rays that come from the wounds of Jesus, and form around Him a mantle of light!

What life is infused into a soul, all at once

* St. Bernard, On Consideration, lib 5, ch iv.

transported into the midst of the infinite, and there drinking in for the first time, at their source, joy and delight!

One language only could express what she felt at this moment — that language with which God speaks to himself internally, through the Spirit and the Word.

LXXXVI.

The Obsequies.

FROM the heights where the soul was triumphing in new happiness, I saw the honors that were given to her body. I was present at the holy ceremonies, and presided. I had blessed the cradle; I was going to bless the tomb.*

From the moment the old man had ceased to live, the tears had redoubled, and the bells, spreading afar their plaintive sound, awoke in all hearts grief that was sincere.

* Life of St. Simon Stylites, Boll.

They did not weep for the just man—they longed for his presence. The mourning was general, each one thought he had sustained a personal loss.*

Around about me began the conversation of intimate friends: " He is no more! What a loss! Did it not seem as if he ought never die? If he is not saved, who will be? Instead of praying for him, we should ask his prayers."

The confidants of his hidden virtues opened their lips for the first time, and told what they had managed to gain from his silence and modesty.

But how incomplete this praise seemed to me, and what other revelations could I not have made! What was most perfect in the eyes of God, remained hid from the sight of men. The world will know one day the wealth of this noble life.

* Life of St Adélard, Ab. of Corbic, Boll.

No one knew how to designate such a death as this. The end of a beautiful day? No; but the end of a beautiful night and the dawn of the only true day. A peaceful sleep here below, followed by a glorious awakening above.

The angels wished to join with men in the homage given to virtue.

Upon the house in which lay the remains of the just man there came to alight a cloud of charming little birds. They gave out melody of a surpassing sweetness, and accompanied it with the joyous fluttering of their wings. Never had colors so vivid captivated the eye; never had voices so sweet delighted the ear. When the crowd gathered they seemed about to fly away: they described a graceful curve in the air, and regained the all-cherished one. It was soon known whence they had come, and what was their country. When they had accomplished their mission in singing the obsequies of the friend of God, they hovered an instant above the earth that covered his body, then suddenly flew up to heaven.*

*Lives of SS. Simon Stylites, Elizabeth of Hungary, George of Clermont, Boll.

LXXXVII.

The Body of the Chosen One.

I LOVE the body of my chosen one. It was part of him, and could not be to me a thing of indifference. The noble instrument of her merits, it will follow the destiny of the soul, and share in it. I will watch over it as a protector and avenger. I will strike fear into the bold that seek to profane it; I will have a thousand favors for those that venerate it.*

To the very trump of resurrection, it will remain intrusted to my keeping. The seal

* St. Theodore Studite, On the Celestial Orders. Lives of SS. Constantine of Peronne, Vincent of Saragossa, Boll.

it bears is indelible. Everywhere I shall recognize those atoms, that were the holocaust of charity, of chastity, of penance, and through which the sacraments gave the supernatural life of grace to the soul.*

In the bosom of the earth and in the abyss of waters, on the wings of the wind and in the perfume of flowers, I follow them with my look.

Whether they mount in the sap of plants, or come open themselves to the sun — whether they sleep beneath the mouldering layers of herbage, or mingle with the dry sand, for me they have the same excellence.

Satan avoids them. They hurt his sight, as bright rays pierce the eyes of the birds of night, and they burn him like hot coals, if he happen to tread them under foot.†

They spread around an odor that attracts the angels, and rejoices them, lifts up the

* St. Ambrose, Serm. 93.
† St Chrysostom, on St Julian, and on the Machabees

hearts of men and makes them better. Those members that were during life subject to infirmity, after death possess the power of driving it away.

I blessed God for deigning thus to honor the dust of my chosen one, while she was yet going through her purgatory in humiliation.

At the last day, when fire shall come to regenerate the world, and when the sound of the trumpet shall burst forth, I shall have a very sweet duty to fulfil. I shall separate from this mass of ashes, the dust, the object of my veneration, and form of it a body that God will clothe with glory.*

In characters of light, sovereign goodness will trace in this body the history of the virtues that were my joy — will adorn it with perfections it did not possess during trial. It will become light, subtle, transparent, and incorruptible. It will have to fear neither

* St Thomas, De Causa Resurr, q 78, art 3.

weakness nor the wrinkles of age. Eternity knows neither age nor decline.

The splendor of the body will be for the elect the complement of their glory. It will make them overflow with happiness unknown to pure spirits. Considering with the eyes of the soul the humanity of the Saviour, they will yet contemplate it with the eyes of the body, and this new sight will be the source of new joys.

From the bosom of God the soul sees on earth the partner of her pilgrimage, and longs to be united to it; but this desire is without impatience, and does not mar her happiness.*

* Louis de Blois, Retraite de l'ame fidele

27 *

LXXXVIII.

The Eternal Union.

WHILE awaiting the confirmation of our glory at the last day, we were enjoying already an unchanging and infinite happiness.

Who can tell the sweetness of an union formed in time to continue in eternity ! *

Not having any longer a ministry of salvation to discharge toward this soul, I did not cease to show her my affection. I still contributed to her happiness by my caresses. I love to seat myself on the same throne, to

* St. Thomas of Villanova, On the Angels.

318

circle my brow with the same crown, to be one heart and one spirit with her.*

I unroll before her eyes the plan of Providence in the work of her sanctification, and trace again the touching picture of my efforts to maintain her in good.

She replies assuring me that this happy past is ever present to her memory, and that these sweet souvenirs are a perfume she breathes with delight.†

Often, in these interviews of love, we leaned one upon the other, under the impulse of a Divine charity, and our hearts received the outpourings of a penetrating joy like to the dew of heaven.

Thus, in the gardens of the earth, men see flowers, side by side, under the beneficent breath of the evening breeze, bend to give each other the kiss of peace, and to mingle their treasures. ‡

* St. Thomas, De Angelis, q 108, art 8. St. Thomas of Villanova, On the Angels

† St. Thomas of Villanova, On the Angels.

‡ Blot, "Au ciel on se reconnait." 6me Lettre

It seems to us that, loving God in ourselves, and loving ourselves in God, the beatitude of this ineffable love grows without ceasing.*

By the mutual union of the angel and of man in the heavens, to God alone, forever be glory, honor, and benediction!!!

* St. Thomas of Villanova, Discourse on St. Michael.

THE END.

CPSIA information can be obtained
at www.ICGtesting.com
Printed in the USA
LVHW081806071122
732532LV00003B/25